I'LL BE HOME FOR CHRISTMAS

COMING HOME FOR CHRISTMAS
BOOK ONE

SYLVIA MCDANIEL

Coming Home for Christmas

I'll Be Home for Christmas
White Christmas
Santa's Baby
All I Want For Christmas
Box Set

A Christmas Miracle in the Snow — Love Comes to the Rescue

Going home for Christmas, Olivia Miller's life takes a sudden, unexpected turn. Stranded in a desolate snow-storm, she's left reeling from a string of losses - her job, her fiance, and now her car. But just when she thought her world couldn't get any colder, rancher Lucas Peterson appears like a guardian angel, rescuing her from the icy clutches of winter.

Lucas, too, is grappling with his own solitary Christmas, haunted by the tragic loss of his parents. As they find themselves drawn together by the forced proximity of the snowstorm, their connection ignites with a passion that defies reason - an insta-love that warms the coldest of hearts.

In this heartwarming holiday tale, Olivia and Lucas discover that sometimes, when life strands you in the snow, it can also lead you to unexpected love and the true meaning of Christmas. Will their love melt away the icy remnants of their pasts and create a new beginning filled with hope, love, and the promise of a brighter future?

CHAPTER 1

As Olivia Miller drove along the highway, the night hurled snow like Mother Nature spewed the white stuff.

The blizzard warnings were right. The wind howled, blowing her little hatchback all over the road while big flakes smacked the windshield like tiny snowballs. What was she doing out in this mess?

Music blared on the radio, and Olivia cringed at the Christmas carol that filled her car, asking for presents, snow, and mistletoe. Mother Nature was delivering on the snow.

"I'll be in Hell for Christmas," she sang, changing the words, tears flowing down her cheeks as she thought about her miserable life.

This day couldn't get much worse.

The holiday season was supposed to be a beautiful,

happy time. A time of love and family, and damn it, this was going to be the worst Christmas ever.

Trying to watch the road, she wiped at the tears that had not stopped flowing since she'd left Billings. She'd waited until the last minute to leave, waiting around for the big jerk since he promised to go with her. And now she was on the road to Whitefish later than she planned. The storm they'd been predicting was upon her. In the dark, she watched as the snowflakes flew in the headlights, the wind shoving from lane to lane, her windshield wipers working overtime to remove snow.

Her sleigh was struggling, and she wasn't feeling jolly, merry, or bright.

For the first time in years, her mother had issued a demand that the family gather at Christmastime for an important announcement, and she'd thought that she and the jerk would be the center of that revelation.

In her mind, she'd dreamed of an engagement ring and a happily ever after with him, asking her in front of her family. Only the dream was a nightmare, and she'd been the only one thinking of a pledge to marry. Not the big jerk.

The only disclosure she'd be making would be that she was still single and alone. That the man she'd thought was Mr. Right was actually Mr. All Wrong. Mr. All Wrong was caught in bed with his coworker. Even now, her eyes had a hard time unseeing the two of them entwined together, naked.

And then there was a second life-changing event that

had come completely out of the blue, taking her by surprise.

The only thing that could be worse would be if she were pregnant. Thank goodness she'd been on the pill. Especially now.

Somewhere her life had taken a wrong turn, and she'd found herself on a road she didn't know how to navigate. Until today, she'd thought that everything was going great. Then life imploded, and everything that could go wrong did, including the job she loved.

Fired.

So what was the family message if not her engagement? She'd not been home since she graduated from college. Time seemed to have gotten away from her, and she'd been focused on the asshole and being the best at her career.

So much for the job and the man she loved.

This was not the first time she'd found a boyfriend cheating on her. What was wrong with her that she seemed to choose men who couldn't keep their dick in their pants?

With a sigh, she wondered how her sisters would react to the news that, once again, she was on her own. Once again, she'd caught her man in bed with someone else. She doubted her siblings ever had problems in regard to men. Especially Amelia, the golden girl.

One of the reasons she avoided going home was that she knew she'd have to deal with her sisters. Why the urgency for the family to spend Christmas together? They'd grown up, and once they reached college, they had become disconnected. By choice.

And now the twins would be there. The favored girls. No, not the oldest woman, but two girls that could do no wrong. Amelia's life was always perfect. Head cheerleader, valedictorian, Mensa member, and scholarship winner.

Now a lawyer.

The family super achiever who probably had never broken a nail, and her hair and makeup were always perfect, and the world awaited her like a queen with her subjects. Bow down to Her Highness.

And Emma was a carbon copy, though she was the introverted twin. Still a super achiever, Emma kept her accomplishments more on the down-low compared to Amelia's shouting from the rooftops. A nurse in the NICU unit, she helped to save babies.

Olivia...she just plodded along, thinking everything was fine, and then she discovered the truth. And nothing was right. None of her decisions, her career, everything gone to hell.

No one would ever call her an overachiever. And she doubted her sisters had ever been fired from their jobs.

The snow was beginning to pile up on the road, and the few cars that had been on the highway suddenly disappeared. It was just her and a truck that had been behind her for the last several miles. When she reached the next town, she would find a hotel and spend the night.

Waiting for the big ass had been a huge mistake, and now she was paying the price in more ways than one. Not only had he cheated on her, but he'd put her so far behind schedule to return home. The plan had been to leave at noon. At five, she gave up and went to his apartment. Mistake number two.

At this rate, she wouldn't make it home tonight. And maybe that was for the best. And yet she needed her mother's hug. It was the reason she'd not completely canceled.

Maybe the two of them could figure out where she'd gone wrong. And there was this supposed family announcement that her mother wanted everyone to hear.

In the white glare of her headlights, her brain realized an elk stood in the middle of the road like the king of the mountains. His size was intimidating and no match for her little car. The damn animal was staring her down, not moving. Her foot immediately moved to the brakes, and when she hit them, her car began to spin on the snowy road.

Mistake number three. Don't slam on the brakes on ice and snow.

With a scream, she turned the wheel in the opposite direction, and when she finally gained control, she saw the snow bank just as her car slammed into it.

Maybe this day could get worse. Her head smashed into the driver's door window, and blackness came rushing toward her. Why had she waited for the big jerk? Why?

CHAPTER 2

ucas Peterson watched the little car spin on the road trying to avoid the elk that had decided it was in his best interest to finish crossing the snowy road. What the car was doing out on a night like this, he had no idea, but when it landed in the snowbank, he knew they were in trouble.

After pulling his four-wheel drive to the side of the road, he hopped out into the cold, sinking to his ankles in snow. The flakes blasted him in the face and he was thankful he wasn't far from home. Pulling his cowboy hat down over his eyes, he approached the semi-buried car.

Yanking open the door, he realized a woman was slumped forward.

"Are you all right?"

She sat back and he saw the blood on her forehead. Glancing at the driver's window, he noted a spider web of cracked glass that had probably been spun when her head connected with the pane. For the first time, he considered she could be seriously hurt.

The woman was beautiful, her sapphire eyes dazed. He wasn't about to move her until he was certain she had mobility in all her limbs.

If she needed an ambulance, it would take hours for them to reach her. Long, cold hours of them trying to stay warm while the storm raged on.

"What a fucking spectacular day," she gasped as she gazed at him, her eyes unfocused.

That was an odd statement.

"Move your fingers and toes," he commanded.

When her eyes teared up, it was all he could do to keep from pulling her into his arms and comforting her. She looked so vulnerable sitting there with her seat belt fastened securely and a trickle of blood on her face.

There was something about her that made him want to console her and tell her everything was going to be all right. That he would not let anything bad happen to her after this moment.

"I'm all right," she said. "Everything is working."

"Show me," he commanded and she moved her fingers and her limbs.

"I just need to get home," she said sniffling.

Sadly, he didn't think she was going to make it tonight. In fact, he didn't know what he was going to do with her. But he couldn't leave her out here in the blizzard.

"Do you need an ambulance?" he asked still wanting to make certain she was unharmed.

"No, just a minor headache," she said, glancing out at her car. "Now what do I do? Can I get out of this mess and continue on?"

"No," he said. "I think your radiator is busted. I smell antifreeze."

He knew what he wanted to do. An air of fragility about her urged him to protect her, keep her safe.

"Noooo," she cried. "My car. My beautiful little car. What else can go wrong today?"

That was a question he couldn't answer because he didn't know what had happened to her. But he could tell she'd been crying.

"I live right down the road," he said. "No one will come out during the storm to tow your car into town. Come with me and you can stay until a tow truck can get you out of the ditch or I can pull you out once it stops snowing. Maybe it will be all right."

That last statement was doubtful, but he wanted to make her feel better. She looked so dejected, completely spent.

Her brows drew down and he figured she was contemplating whether it was a good idea to go with a total stranger. And with the way the world was today, he couldn't blame her.

"This storm has just started. No one is getting out in this weather. In fact, the state police are telling everyone to stay off the roads," he told her. It was true, they had issued the warning less than an hour ago. "You'll be safe at my house. Here in the car, you'll freeze to death. As soon as we can, we'll get someone to pull your car out."

"I don't know you," she said and winced as she reached up and touched her head in the spot where she'd hit the side window.

It was a valid concern, but she could either choose him or stay here and freeze to death.

"I don't know you either," he said. "But I'm not going to let you freeze to death out here in this weather. Until this blizzard passes, we can be strangers sharing a house. You can stay on one side of the house and I'll stay on the other."

Just then a blast of snow and ice hit him and he had to hang onto the car. The weather was quickly deteriorating. They needed to get home before the snow blocked the road to his house.

Though he knew she was not going to like what he was doing, he had no choice.

Gazing at her, he reached into the car, unbuckled her seat belt, and lifted her out.

"Hey," she said. "I haven't said whether I'm going with you or not."

"Darling, we're running out of time. This road is going to be impassable soon. Time to go or we'll both be stuck trying to survive a snowstorm. That's not how I want to spend the next few days."

He carried her through the snow, opened the passenger door of his truck, and set her inside. She'd felt soft in his arms and he liked the way she smelled of Christmas cookies, reminding him of his mother.

He had the most incredible urge to kiss her, but that would frighten her.

"My purse and phone are still in the car," she said. "I need to call my family and tell them where I am."

Nodding, he walked back through the accumulating snow. They would have three feet by morning. Reaching inside, he grabbed her purse, phone, and keys to the car that had died on impact.

Then he hurried back to his truck.

When he stepped inside, he handed her everything and then pulled the truck away from the side of the road. The headlights showed the snow was coming down harder. They would be doing good to make it to his ranch.

Glancing at her, he could see she was nervous and he couldn't blame her. Times were dangerous for women, but she had nothing to fear from him.

And he knew when they arrived at his ranch, she would not like the idea that they were alone.

"Where were you headed?"

"Whitefish," she said with a sigh. "My parents are expecting me. I need to let them know I'm going to be late."

What the hell was she doing out so late on the road going to Whitefish? She was still three hours away.

"Why didn't you leave earlier?"

A big sigh came from her and he knew something had held her up. "The plan was to leave at noon. I got held up until five. And now it appears I don't know when I'll get there."

He wondered what had kept her from leaving. But that was none of his business unless she wanted to tell him.

"When we get to the house, why don't you call your family? You can use my phone if yours doesn't work. Mine works most of the time," he said. "I've got a booster antenna for it on the house."

Sometimes the weather kept his phone from working, but he hoped for her sake that she could reach her family. Certainly that would make her feel better. At least then someone she knew would know of her whereabouts.

Turning onto the dirt road that led to his ranch, he had to be careful or they could get stuck. The snow was deep and the mud was frozen.

Putting the truck into four-wheel drive, they began the sloppy trek down the lane slipping and sliding through the snow. When he reached the gate, she gazed at the large wooden entry. "Peterson's Folly."

He grinned at her. "I'm Lucas Peterson by the way. I'd shake your hand, but right now I need both on the wheel."

"Olivia Miller," she said. "Why is your ranch called Peterson's Folly?"

Gazing at her, he smiled as he recanted his family history.

"My grandfather had a racehorse named Folly and he won enough money that he was able to purchase this spread. It's been in the family for generations."

And now he was the only family member left. Sadness gripped him, but he pushed the feelings away. Now was not the time or there might be no family left after tonight.

The automatic gate tried to swing open through the snow and he knew it wasn't going to make it. "Excuse me."

He jumped out of the truck and the snow came up mid-calf. Pushing the gate open manually, he had to move some of the snow out of the way with a shovel he kept chained to the gate.

When the snow was deep, the tool came in handy.

Once he'd moved enough snow, he climbed back in.

This was the first big snowstorm of the season. Sure, they had several inches before, but this storm was going to make feet, not inches.

"Don't be surprised if we get snowed in for a couple of days," he said, putting the truck back in gear. Thank goodness the cattle trucks had hauled away most of the herd several weeks ago. The remaining heads were close to the house and he could feed them hay.

"No," she said. "I have to be in Whitefish for Christmas."

Stealing a peek at her, he could see she was visibly upset at the idea of not getting to her family before the holiday. "We'll see what happens."

Whitefish was still several hours away and the roads were already covered with more snow coming down. The plows would not be out until the precipitation stopped and then they would see how much damage the little vehicle had sustained.

It was not looking good for her to make it to Whitefish before Christmas.

As they neared the house, she saw the Christmas lights that twinkled different colors on his ranch house.

The lights always filled him with warmth and happiness, even though his mother was no longer around.

"Oh, this is beautiful," she said. "Who put up the lights? Your parents?"

Now she was about to learn they would be alone.

"No," he said, "I put them up."

His mother had loved the house to be adorned for Christmas, and in honor of her memory, he made certain their home was decorated just the way she would've liked.

It always filled him with pleasure at the thought of how happy she'd be to see he'd kept up the tradition. But secretly, he wished she was here hanging Christmas lights and giving the family direction on how she wanted everything.

Olivia frowned at him. "You do have family living with you?"

He licked his dry lips. "No. My parents are both dead. I gave the servants the week off to spend with their families. We're going to be all alone."

Until now, he'd planned on being by himself for the holidays.

A gasp came from her and she shook her head. "No."

"If you want me to, I'll go stay in the barn," he said, knowing it would be a cold night, but at least she might feel more comfortable. And he wanted her to trust him. He would never hurt her, but she didn't know that beneath his cowboy hat was just a lonely man.

Biting her bottom lip, he could see that she was indecisive. "No, it would be too cold."

"Good," he said. "I was not looking forward to bedding down with the cattle. Don't worry, I'm not a serial killer or a rapist or a bad person. Just a lonely cowboy."

Her brows drew together. "You're a stranger," she said. "And yet, I don't know what I would have done if you hadn't stopped."

As the truck pulled up in front of the house, he didn't answer her, but feared she would have frozen to death.

"We're two strangers brought together by a bad storm."

CHAPTER 3

Olivia sat in the truck that Lucas had pulled beneath an awning in front of the house.

"Let me help you out," he said as he crawled from the truck. When he reached her side, he opened the door and assisted her down.

"I'm really all right," she said just as her knees buckled beneath her.

While she felt fine, the emotional trauma from the day was starting to get to her. It was like everything that could go wrong had, and now she reeled from the emotional day.

"Sure you are," he said. "No ambulance can make it out here tonight, so don't grow weak on me now."

A sigh escaped her. "This really has been a colossal bad day."

He didn't say anything as he walked beside her holding onto her elbow in a gentle manner. Through his gloved fingers, strength resonated from his fingertips. Warmth filled her and she was stunned at the way the big cowboy seemed to hover over her to protect her, holding her to keep her from falling.

Christmas decorations lined the sidewalk leading up to the big wooden front door with a big wreath. She groaned at the sight, knowing it was doubtful that she'd make it home to Whitefish, to her family, and the big announcement that her mother had insisted they come home for.

When Lucas opened the front door, she glanced into the house and saw all the Christmas decorations filling the log cabin. They were gorgeous, but it was just another reminder of what she'd gone through today.

A groan escaped from between her lips. Not even her mother put up this much at Christmas. Yet it was beautiful, even if she didn't want to celebrate. She had no reason to be happy, jolly, and filled with good cheer.

Lucas shot her a look. "Are you all right?"

"Yes," she said, wondering if he was going to treat her like fine china the rest of the night. But after today, would that be a bad thing?

Standing in the hallway, she gazed into the big room with a tall Christmas tree sparkling with white lights and glass bulbs hanging on the limbs and tinsel. Decorations were scattered about the room.

It looked like someone had puked Christmas all around the room, and while normally she'd be thrilled, after today, it was just a reminder of everything she'd thought she'd receive for Christmas and wasn't.

"Oh, you're a grinch," he said.

Hardly. She was the teacher who had gone out of her way to make certain her students had a little something for Christmas. No, she didn't use to be a grinch or Scrooge or even a grumpy Christmas person, but sometimes life interfered, and this year, she was spinning from the interference.

Turning, she faced him. "No, I'm not a grinch. I'm a realist, and right now, my Christmas spirit is badly bruised."

"We'll have to change that," he said smiling at her.

Good luck with that.

She didn't want anyone to make her feel better. She felt like she had the right to hate Christmas and everything else in her life at the moment.

"Let me show you to your room," he said.

"Where are you sleeping?" she asked, nerves filling her.

"I'm on the other side of the house. The guest quarters are on this side," he said. "But if you need me, I'm not far."

Oh no, she didn't need a man, though Lucas was very handsome in the light. His big brown eyes and long dark lashes were an enticement, but not one she was going to be tempted to try.

At the moment, she almost hated the opposite sex. But it wasn't Lucas's fault that someone had kicked her to the curb in spectacular fashion with a woman in his bed.

"Currently, we have electricity, but this storm could take it down anytime. I'd suggest if you're going to take a shower, you grab one now before we lose hot water," he said.

Taking her elbow, he led her up the stairs. She couldn't help but wonder if it would be wise for her to take a shower since they were alone. Maybe he was a Boy Scout, but her trust in men was shredded. She didn't trust anyone.

And yet she didn't get bad vibes from Lucas, but sensed a sweetness about him she wasn't quite expecting. It was like he wanted to make certain she was all right. That she was comfortable with him.

It wasn't like she had much of a choice on whether to stay or leave. But right now, she'd just like to be left alone to do her grieving without sharing her feelings with a stranger.

He led her to a bedroom with a queen-size bed and its own private bathroom. The guest room was nice and the perfect place for her to stay. But she didn't want to be here.

"You should have everything you need in the bathroom. I'm going to take a shower now in case we lose power. When you're finished, come down to the big room," he said. "I'll fix us some dinner."

She nodded and watched as he walked out the door. Then she turned and gazed at the room. With a sigh, she took her purse into the bathroom. She tried to call her parents and all she got was a fast busy signal.

Instead, she sent her parents a quick text hoping they would receive it and not worry about her, plus, someone else would know she was at Peterson's Folly Ranch.

There were stories of women disappearing and never being seen again, and she often wondered what happened to them. Could they have been rescued on a snowy night?

With a sigh, she removed her clothes before she crawled into the shower, wishing she'd thought to bring her suitcase with her. But then again, right now her head ached and she'd been barely conscious of what was going on.

Before starting the water, she locked the bathroom door. No, it wasn't much of a deterrent. If he really wanted in, he could simply bust the door down. When the warm spray hit her, she couldn't help but enjoy the way the water felt against her skin. This morning's shower seemed like a week ago.

Even this afternoon felt like days ago.

When she finished, she stepped out and grabbed a towel. Glancing around, she sighed. She had nothing clean to wear.

After opening the bathroom door to the bedroom, she noticed a pair of flannel pajamas on the bed. Lucas had brought her something to wear.

At least flannel pj's were not sexy or enticing.

Putting on the pajamas, she noticed they smelled like Lucas and her heart beat a little faster. These must be his and she pulled them up almost to her breast to keep them from pooling around her ankles. With one last glance in the mirror, she noticed her head oozed blood again.

The cut was high next to her hairline, and hopefully, it wouldn't leave a scar.

After grabbing a couple of aspirin from her purse, she tried her parents' phone one more time. Not even a signal. She headed downstairs, feeling extremely self-conscious in his pj's. Yet she enjoyed the feel of the flannel against her skin.

Glancing at the Christmas decorations, she tried to shake her grouchiness. This was her favorite time of the year, and yet she'd had one of the worst days she could ever remember.

It wasn't often you were fired from your job, found your boyfriend in bed with a coworker, and then had a freakish wreck that damaged your car and had you spending the night with a stranger.

A very handsome stranger.

CHAPTER 4

After Lucas laid the pair of pajamas on her bed, he'd hurried to get his own shower, knowing the electricity would go down soon. While he had a backup generator, there was no telling how long before they had regular service again, and he hated to put a strain on his generator that would make certain they stayed warm and were able to cook.

Outside the window, the wind howled.

Stepping into the shower, he sighed as the warm water pelted him.

Standing beneath the spray, all he could think about was the woman on the other side of his home. He'd been alone for so long and it was nice to have company. Especially, a beautiful woman like Olivia who he'd felt an immediate attraction to.

The urge to shield her and make her his was undeniable. But he wouldn't do anything that would cause her alarm.

Why she'd been out driving in this storm, he had no idea, but when he'd seen her little car trying to stop before it hit the elk, he'd known she was going into the ditch. And when he'd seen that her head hit the window, he'd been worried.

A big ambulance would have trouble maneuvering on unplowed roads, even with chains on the tires. And with the strong winds and blowing snow, a helicopter could not have rescued her.

He was thankful she was not hurt any worse. But the damage to her car was going to be bad.

She appeared to be a very strong-willed woman. There was a sadness that emanated from her sapphire eyes. And now she would be sleeping under his roof. At least until the storm passed and they were able to get her car moved by a wrecker.

It had been so long since he'd dated. He'd not been out on the town since his family had passed away. Life could turn in an instant and leave you alone. Leave you with no one to spend the holidays with. Leave you in a big ranch house that held so many memories of his parents and his sister, of them running down the stairs at Christmas.

Memories of the laughter and the happiness that he missed.

When Olivia walked through his front door, he'd envisioned her laughing before the Christmas tree, her belly rounded with his child. Shaking his head, he cleared his thoughts. He'd just met her, and yet immediately, he'd felt a connection.

A connection, but that didn't mean he was ready to wire into her sockets and live happily ever after. Right now, he was just helping her in a desperate situation.

The thought of her on the other side of the house, naked in his shower, had his breath catching. Oh yes, that damn connection had him thinking about her in sexual ways. Exactly what she didn't need at this moment.

Reaching down, his hand closed around his cock and he sighed. Olivia was a temptation fate had delivered, and he wasn't going to screw this up. It had been so long, and he could see the fear in her eyes. Better to take care of his cock now than to let her see that he'd been instantly attracted to her.

Besides, this was his life. Alone, jerking off in the shower. But at least tonight, he had a face and a body to imagine as he gripped his penis and envisioned Olivia's full breasts and long legs wrapped around him. Her sweet, full red lips that he longed to taste. The feel of her breasts crushed against his chest as he pounded into her.

Somehow he needed to make her feel at ease, and walking around with a hard-on would only freak her out. She had nothing to worry about from him, but she didn't know that. She didn't know he was a good man who respected women and only wanted to find true love. To spend his life beside one woman, honoring and loving her and raising a family.

Children. To have laughter and joy filling this house once again.

Throwing his head back, he moaned as he came alone in the shower. This was his life and he was tired of having no one to share his day with. No one to talk to about his dreams or create a family with. The big ol' house echoed with the memories of his family.

He turned the water off, grabbed a towel, and quickly dried off. The lights flickered and he felt certain the power would soon go out.

Pulling on a pair of warm pajamas, he took a deep breath and walked into the living room. She sat on his couch frowning at her phone, her long dark hair tumbled forward covering her face.

"I can't get through to my parents," she said. "They'll be worried sick."

"Try with my phone," he said. "I'm hooked up to the antenna we have here on the property. Hopefully, you can get through on it."

She glanced up at him, her sapphire eyes gazing at him with a little less trepidation. Hopefully she would soon relax and realize she had nothing to fear from him. In reality, he was the one who actually had everything to fear from her because he wanted a woman in his life. If he became attached to her, she would break his heart and that thought scared the hell out of him.

Was he so lonely that the first woman to come along he was drawn to? Was he so lonely that he would jump at the chance for romance with just anyone?

No, he refused to feel that way after the last woman had broken off their engagement. This time he was going to be certain.

He'd endured enough pain in the last year. It was time for him to experience happiness again.

She reached up and took the phone from him and quickly dialed her parent's number.

"Mom," she said.

"Where are you?" he heard her mother ask, panic in her voice.

"The car is in a ditch," she said with a whimper. "But I'm okay and I'm staying—"

In that moment, the power died, and in the darkness, he watched her face crumble. Frantically, she redialed.

"No, no, no," she cried redialing over and over again. The phone was dead.

The generator came on and she handed the phone back to him and covered her face. He'd seen the tears and his chest ached at the sight.

"Hey, what's wrong? You're safe, you're warm, and you can stay here as long as you need to," he said. "At least your mother knows you're safe."

She made a big gulping noise and he knew the sobs were seconds away. What would he do with a crying woman? Tears were something that always got to him.

Reaching out, he pulled her to her feet against his chest. She needed comforting.

"It's been a horrible day," she said as the tears seemed to

overwhelm her. "Everything went wrong. This is the worst Christmas ever."

CHAPTER 5

$\mathcal{E}$verything that happened today overwhelmed her and the tears came tumbling down her cheeks fast and furious. Sure she'd cried over the big jerk earlier, but this time it was the cumulation of everything.

Being fired, catching her cheating boyfriend, her car landing in a ditch, and now the damn phone not working to let her mother know she was fine.

Sobbing, she leaned against this stranger's warm chest. "I got fired from my teaching job this morning. I read a Christmas story to the children that one of the parents objected to and they fired me."

The tears came faster. She'd loved her students. Seeing their bright, eager, shiny faces each morning had been a joy and she loved teaching. And when one of the children asked her to read the story, she hadn't hesitated. It was a lovely Christmas story, but someone objected and now she was unemployed.

"I'm sorry," he said patting her on the back.

"My mother insisted we all come home for Christmas this year," she said sobbing. "I thought my ex had planned to ask me to marry him in front of my family."

The memory of seeing him this afternoon made the tears come faster. The pain of his deception was almost more than she could bear.

"We were supposed to leave at noon," she said. "I kept waiting for him to come over. I called him. I texted him, and finally, I drove over to his apartment."

She cried even harder. That had been mistake number one. You never went over to your boyfriend's apartment to wait on him, only to discover he was too busy entertaining to let you know he had changed his mind.

Lucas's hand was on her back and he rubbed in a comforting way. "It's okay."

"I had a key to his apartment, and when I walked in, I found him in bed with one of his coworkers. He said he had planned to call me and tell me we were breaking up, but just hadn't done it because he and Cynthia were in bed having sex."

She sobbed. "I thought he was going to ask me to marry him. I thought we were happy. He said he loved me and wanted to meet my family. And then I find him in bed with another woman."

Hiccupping, the tears kept coming. "I'd been waiting for him all afternoon and he'd been in bed with Cynthia. It was after five when I left. Traffic was bad getting out of Billings and then the storm arrived. I was so scared and when I saw the elk standing in the road, I hit the brakes too hard and slid into the snowbank. My car is probably totaled, I have no job, and now no boyfriend. Plus, Christmas with my family can be trying. And yet, my mother wants us all together for the holidays."

The thought of being around the super twins had her crying even harder. Especially since she thought she would receive an engagement ring for Christmas, and instead, she was stuck in a stranger's home.

"How can I be happy and cheerful when I just destroyed my life," she said.

"I'm sorry," Lucas said. "You really did have a bad day. But he didn't respect you. My father raised me to honor and respect women. And that man didn't do either. You deserve someone much better. You deserve a man who will love you and take care of you and your children. You may not think so right now, but you dodged a bullet. A marital nightmare."

While his words were comforting, she continued to cry.

"Right now, teachers are so vulnerable and parents don't realize that without teachers their children are not going to go very far in this world. You need to find a school district that will support you and have your back. You're teaching the next generation, and you shouldn't be taken for granted. That school district did you no favors."

Oh, how she was going to miss her students. She'd loved them. And even the principal, Mrs. Stewart, had cried when she said she had to let her go. The school board was backing the parents even though they believed the book she'd read to her class had not been bad. But they were afraid of the parents and so it was just easier to let her go. Why fight when she could be replaced?

Now her teaching career had a stain on it, though Mrs. Stewart promised to give her glowing reviews. Did the parents not understand what this did to a teacher? Maybe their home lives were the reason, but regardless, she'd cared for each and every one of them.

His arms were wrapped around her and she realized her breasts were crushed against his chest and it felt good. When had the asshat ever held her like this or comforted her like Lucas was? Promised her she would find something better?

She gave a little hiccup, but the tears were finally starting to slow down.

"How is your head feeling?"

"It's throbbing," she said, realizing she'd never taken the aspirin.

"Let's sit you down at the table. I'll put some antibiotic cream on the gash and give you some aspirin. Then we'll put an ice pack on it," he said. "I also need to make certain your eyes aren't dilated."

The man was a stranger and yet he'd cared more about her than her ex.

"With as much crying as I've done this afternoon, I'm surprised my eyes are still working."

Leaning back, she saw the wet spot on his pajamas at his shoulder where her tears had flowed. "I'm so sorry. I soaked your shirt."

He reached out and ran his hand through her hair. "It's all right. After the day you've had, it was probably good for you to have a therapeutic cry. Let's take care of that wound. Then if you're hungry, I'll feed you some soup."

Taking her by the hand, he led her into the kitchen and guided her to the table. First, he gave her two aspirin and a glass of water. She quickly downed them, hoping they would ease the pounding in her head.

Watching him, he hovered around her.

Reaching into a drawer, he found a small flashlight and gazed into her eyes.

"Your pupils are reactive and dilate, so I think you're okay," he said. "But I don't think you should go to sleep right away. Let's keep you up for a while to see if you do all right."

It made sense, but frankly, she still just wanted to lie in bed and cry herself to sleep.

Next, he took a first aid kit from a drawer. After wiping her head with a towelette, he put antibiotic cream on the cut and covered it with a bandage.

"There, now you're all set unless you start to feel bad. Let's hope you start feeling better," he said.

Sitting there, she watched him move around the kitchen and wondered why he was alone. He'd said he gave his servants the week off. But where was his family? And why wasn't he married?

"My housekeeper made me some homemade chicken noodle soup. Are you hungry?"

She'd had nothing since breakfast, so she should probably eat.

"Yes," she said. "It's been a long time since this morning."

"Good," he said handing her an ice pack. "You sit right there and I'll warm us up some food."

As she watched him fix her a bowl, she couldn't help but think how this kind, gentle man was taking care of her – a stranger. Part of her thought it was just a set-up and soon she'd be fighting him off, but the kinder, gentler side of her was staring at him in appreciation.

What would it be like to be Lucas's girlfriend? Shaking her head, she knew that couldn't happen because it was way too soon after being dumped.

Thinking back on the men in her life, she realized that no one had ever taken care of her like Lucas. When she had the flu, the boyfriend's response had been "stay home, don't come see me and I hope you get to feeling better soon."

The least he could have done was bring her food or go to the store and get her medications. But no, he'd been afraid of contracting her disease as he liked to call it.

When they finished the delicious soup, Lucas smiled at her.

"Feeling better?"

"Yes," she said realizing the aspirin and even the cold pack had helped with her headache.

"Good," he said as he stood to gather the used dishes.

"Let me help you," she said feeling like she should do

something instead of just sitting there taking advantage of his kindness.

"No," he said. "You need to rest tonight. Why don't we sit in the living room and I'll build a fire to help the generator warm the house."

She nodded and he helped her walk into the living room.

"I think I'm going to be all right," she said. "You don't have to help me."

"Tonight, I want to make certain you don't get dizzy or fall. Let me pamper you," he said.

What boyfriend had ever said that to her? None.

As she sat on the sofa, he laid a soft blanket beside her. "In case you get chilled."

She pulled it up over her legs and sighed.

After he had lit the fire in the huge rock fireplace, she gazed at him sitting so far away in a recliner. It was like he was trying to make her feel comfortable around him. And she was glad.

So far, he'd not made any moves on her and for that she was grateful.

"Now that I've cried all over you and gotten your pajamas wet telling you about my bad day, tell me about yourself. How long have you lived here all alone?"

CHAPTER 6

ow. No wonder Olivia hadn't smiled at his Christmas decorations.

She'd lost everything today, her job, her boyfriend, her sense of direction, and she was still standing. Barely. But standing nonetheless.

Lucas admired that kind of strength. Even through her tears, she hadn't folded. She hadn't collapsed. She'd leaned on him, yes, but she hadn't shattered.

And now, watching her sitting curled up on his couch, wrapped in one of his old blankets, a faint flush returning to her cheeks, he felt something he hadn't felt in a long time.

Hope.

Not just hope that she'd be okay.

Hope that maybe, someday, he might not be alone anymore.

But tonight wasn't about him. It was about her.

She needed comfort. Safety. Warmth. Not another complicated man with baggage.

Still, when she looked up at him and asked about his past, something loosened in his chest.

Maybe it wouldn't hurt to tell her a little.

"My family's been ranching here since before Montana was even a state," he began, his voice low and steady. "My great-grandparents came out here with nothing but a stubborn mule and a dream. My great-grandfather bought a racehorse named Folly that turned out to be a real winner. He bet everything on her, won big, and used the money to buy this land."

Lucas knew he was fortunate. He was wealthy because of his ancestors who had survived some of the worst blizzards and still made this ranch successful. In the morning, he would need to take hay out to the cattle even in the snow.

But that was a small price to pay for the life he led.

She smiled. "That's a hell of a story."

He nodded, leaning back in the recliner. "We've been raising cattle ever since. At our peak, we run over a thousand head in the summer. But winters are brutal, so I sell off most of the herd and keep around two hundred pregnant cows close to the house."

Her eyes widened. "That sounds like an enormous operation. Do you have help?"

He hesitated. This was the part he never quite knew how to explain.

"My parents passed away last year," he said, keeping his voice even. "It's just me now."

Her lips parted slightly, sympathy flooding her expression. "I'm so sorry."

He nodded once. "Thanks. I've got a couple of hands who come out during the day, and a housekeeper who helps when she can. But I like the quiet. Most of the time."

There was a pause. Then she tilted her head.

"Is your girlfriend okay with me staying here?" she asked, teasing just enough to lighten the moment. "Because if I were her, I'd be raising an eyebrow."

A short laugh escaped him. "No girlfriend. Hasn't been for over a year."

In fact, she'd deserted him a week after his family died. And yet, he felt grateful. Because if she didn't care enough to be concerned with him dealing with grief, then there was no place for her in his life.

Her expression turned curious. "Let me guess. She couldn't handle the country life?"

He gave a dry smile. "Exactly. City girl. Loved the idea of a cowboy—hated the reality of mud, manure, and early mornings."

"Her loss," Olivia said quietly.

Their eyes met across the room, and something passed between them—unspoken but tangible.

"You've had a dry spell," she said. "Lucky you."

"Yes, ma'am, I have," he said. "I'm very picky when it comes to women. For me, I want a marriage like my parents had. They were each other's universe and they had each other's backs. They were first in each other's worlds and loved one another until death separated them."

She stretched her legs out on the couch and pulled the blanket up closer. A gust of wind slammed into the house, and for a moment, the lights flickered, but the generator continued.

"That storm is not getting any weaker," she said with a sigh.

"No," he said. "I'll give you a flashlight before we go to bed, in case the generator fails."

"Thank you," she said. "How long were your parents married?"

"Thirty-five years," he said. "The first years, they were separated because my father was in the service. When he came home, my mother got pregnant with me. How about your family?"

Lucas cleared his throat and shifted in his seat. "What about you? You mentioned sisters?"

She groaned softly. "The golden girls. Amelia and Emma. One's a lawyer, the other's a NICU nurse. They save babies and win awards and never get caught crying in strangers' living rooms."

He chuckled. "Sounds exhausting."

She grinned. "It is. Amelia was head cheerleader, valedictorian, and a scholarship winner. Emma is quieter but no less perfect. I was the artsy one. The messy one. The teacher who barely scraped through college."

"You're also the one who makes kids feel seen. The one who reads to them and helps them believe in stories."

Her throat bobbed. She blinked at him, eyes suddenly glassy again—but not from fresh tears.

"Thank you," she said, her voice soft. "You're the first person who's said that."

He leaned forward, resting his elbows on his knees. "It's true. You were doing what you love. That takes guts."

"You're going to find a better teaching job than the one you had. And the students will love you."

She bit her lip and it was all he could do to keep from groaning. "I hope so."

He had to change the subject and get her mind on something else.

She stared at the fire, her voice distant. "I thought I had my life figured out. I was going to teach, get married, maybe write children's books someday."

Lucas perked up. "You want to write books?"

Her gaze turned toward him, a little sheepish. "Yeah. Someday. My students used to tell me what kinds of stories they wanted to hear, and I started jotting down ideas. I don't know if I'll ever get there, but... it's a dream."

"I think you should chase it."

"Easy for you to say, cowboy," she said, teasing again. "You've got a thousand acres of land and a legacy."

He gave a self-deprecating shrug. "It's a lot of cows and a lot of snow."

She laughed, a soft, melodic sound that filled the room like music. It made his heart lurch in his chest.

"What was your favorite book growing up?" she asked, tucking her feet beneath her.

He leaned back, smiling. "Pirate stories. My mom used to read to me every night. She'd go to the library and bring home stacks of books about buried treasure and stormy seas. I didn't even like reading until she made it an adventure."

Olivia sighed. "That sounds amazing."

"What about you?"

"*Little Women*," she said without hesitation. "Jo March was my hero."

"Let me guess—you're a Jo."

"Is there anyone who doesn't want to be Jo?" she said, stretching and stifling a yawn. "Although... I wouldn't have turned down a Laurie."

He laughed. "Remind me to dig out my top hat."

She laughed again, then yawned again—this one longer, her eyes glassy with exhaustion.

Lucas stood and tossed another log onto the fire. Sparks crackled up the chimney.

"You should probably get some sleep," he said gently.

She nodded, rubbing her eyes. "Yeah. That's probably a good idea."

He grabbed the flashlight from the side table. "Let me check your eyes one more time, just to be safe."

She rolled her eyes but smiled. "You're very persistent."

"I'm nothing if not thorough."

He crouched in front of her and gently shined the light into her eyes. Her pupils reacted normally.

Shining the light in her eyes, her pupils reacted normally.

"You're in the clear," he said. "Still breathing. Still beautiful."

That last part slipped out before he could stop it.

Her gaze flicked to his, surprised... but not offended.

In fact, she blushed.

He handed her the flashlight. "Just in case the generator kicks off tonight. I'll be up around six to feed the animals, but I'll be quiet. If you feel up to it, you can join me. If not, enjoy sleeping in."

Her brow furrowed. "How do you feed cattle in a snowstorm?"

"I've got a sleigh rigged up with runners," he said. "I load it with hay, hook it to the snowmobile, and make rounds through the pens. It's cold, but it works."

"That sounds... kind of magical."

He smiled. "Some days. Most days it's just cold."

Another yawn escaped her, and she stood, the blanket falling away as she stretched. His pajama pants looked adorable on her, too long, cinched high on her waist, the sleeves of the shirt swallowing her hands. And yet, somehow, she looked like she belonged in them.

"Thank you for everything, Lucas," she said. "You've been... incredible."

"You're welcome. Sleep well, Olivia. And just so you know, you're safe here. I'll be on the other side of the house, nowhere near your door."

Her expression softened. "I know. You've made that clear."

He hesitated, watching her walk toward the staircase. She paused, glanced back at him.

"I'm really glad you stopped tonight," she said quietly.

"So am I," he said.

And then, like a dream, she disappeared up the stairs.

Lucas stood there for a moment, the fire crackling behind him, the scent of cedarwood and cinnamon lingering in the air.

He ran a hand through his hair, exhaled hard, and finally turned away.

Because as much as he wanted to follow her up those stairs, kiss her, carry her to bed... he wouldn't.

She needed time.

But she wasn't just another beautiful woman who needed rescuing.

She was something else entirely.

She was *real*.

And he already knew, deep in his bones, that Olivia Miller wasn't just a stranded stranger.

She was the storm that might change everything.

CHAPTER 7

The scent of coffee drifted through the air like a gentle invitation.

Olivia stirred beneath the warm flannel sheets, blinking in the soft morning light that spilled through the tall windows. For a moment, she wasn't sure where she was. Then she remembered—the crash, the storm, the stranger.

Lucas.

She turned her head, looking at the wooden chair she'd wedged beneath the doorknob the night before.

Still in place. Unmoved.

Relief whispered through her body. So far, Lucas had done nothing but prove he was exactly what he claimed to be: a decent, kind, respectful man.

A rarity.

She hadn't meant to fall asleep so quickly last night, but exhaustion and emotion had taken her under like a wave. Her headache was gone now, her body rested, and her first thought wasn't of the crash or the storm, but of him.

His voice.

His quiet strength.

The way he'd held her when she cried.

She rose from bed and padded into the bathroom, splashing cold water on her face. Her cheeks were a bit pale, her eyes still slightly puffy from the tears, but she didn't look broken. She looked like someone rebuilding.

After dressing in yesterday's clothes, still crumpled but dry, she moved the chair aside and cracked the bedroom door.

The house was silent except for the hum of the generator and the soft clink of dishes in the kitchen.

Crossing into the living room, she paused at the large picture window and stared out at the Montana landscape now fully blanketed in white. Snow was still falling in lazy drifts, but the flakes were smaller, less urgent. Maybe the worst had passed.

She was shocked at the Christmas decorations in the house. Had he done the decorating or had his house-keeper? She'd ask him about that as well. There were things about him that she found intriguing, and she wanted to learn the answers.

Stretching, she thought about yesterday and sighed. The worst was being fired from the job she loved. But as far as the jerk was concerned, she was better off without him.

If only she hadn't waited so late to leave, she would

have awoken in her childhood home this morning surrounded by her family, and right now, she was missing them.

While she was looking forward to seeing her parents, she dreaded the reunion with the golden girls. Their lives were perfect while hers was a complete disaster. And having to listen to them talk about their success would only make her sad.

She stared out the window and sighed. The weather had taken her plans, stomped on them, and buried them under four feet of snow.

Everything outside was muted. Quiet. Like the whole world was holding its breath.

She stepped into the kitchen, drawn toward the source of the warm, earthy aroma. A fresh pot of coffee steamed on the counter. She poured a mug and stood there, cradling it in both hands, letting the heat seep into her fingers.

Then she spotted him.

Through the window, she saw Lucas in the distance, bundled up in winter gear, riding a snowmobile across the yard. The attached wooden sled was now empty of hay. He must've just finished feeding the cattle.

She watched as he parked the vehicle near the barn, climbed off, and immediately sank knee-deep into the snow. Unfazed, he trudged into the barn, disappearing for a few moments before reappearing, this time on snow-shoes. Clever. He detached the sled, pulled it into the barn, then turned and started back toward the house.

Even from a distance, there was something about the way he moved. Confident. Capable. At ease with the land. The kind of man who didn't need to make loud declarations, his actions spoke for him.

A few minutes later, she heard the outer door open. The muffled thump of boots hitting the floor. The sounds of someone removing layers, shaking off snow.

Then he stepped into the kitchen, cheeks and nose red from the cold, his dark hair tousled beneath a knit hat, and his brown eyes lighting up when he saw her.

"Good morning," he said, unzipping his coat and hanging it on the back of a chair. "How are you feeling?"

"No headache," she said. "No soreness. And... really good, actually."

He smiled, and it made her heart skip a beat. How did he manage to look both rugged and gentle at the same time?

"Glad to hear it. Did you sleep okay?"

She nodded, sipping her coffee. "Out like a light."

She didn't mention the chair at the door. He didn't need to know about the lingering shadows of her mistrust.

Not when he'd given her no reason to doubt him.

She let her gaze linger on him. His sandy hair was damp with snowmelt, his flannel shirt hugged his shoulders, and those eyes, *God*, those eyes, were the kind that looked straight into you and didn't flinch.

Yes, Lucas Peterson was... very handsome. And very hard not to stare at.

"I wish we'd thought to grab my suitcase," she said. "It would be nice to change into clean clothes."

"I was thinking about that," he said, leaning casually against the counter. "Once we eat, I can take the snowmobile back out to the highway. We'll check on your car, leave a note for the highway patrol, and see if we can grab your things."

Her heart lifted. "Really? You'd do that?"

He nodded. "I don't think the truck can make it through the snow yet, but the sled'll get us there. I won't try to plow until the storm stops for good. No point in wasting fuel."

Something about the way he spoke, calm, practical, thoughtful, eased her nerves. He wasn't rushing her. Wasn't pushing her. He was simply *there*.

"Thank you," she said softly.

"Of course." He gave her a once-over. "You'll need warmer clothes, though. You'd freeze in what you've got on."

He hesitated. "I think you could wear some of Grace's gear."

"You have a sister?" she asked.

A shadow passed over his face. "Had. She passed last year. Along with the rest of my family."

He turned away before she could respond, reaching for the skillet.

Her stomach twisted. She hadn't meant to bring up painful memories.

"I'm sorry," she said quietly.

He didn't respond right away. When he did, his voice

was steady. "It's okay. I don't mind telling you later. Just... not first thing in the morning."

She understood that kind of pain. The kind that needed space.

"Why are you doing all this?" she asked suddenly. "Helping me like this? Taking care of me?"

Whirling around, he took a step closer to her, and her heart beat faster in her chest.

He faced her fully, his expression unguarded. "Because you deserve to be treated well. Because you've had a rough time. And because I believe people are supposed to help each other when they can."

Then he stepped closer and took her hand in his.

Her breath caught.

"I may live out here in the middle of nowhere," he said, "but I'm not a monster. You're safe here, Olivia. You always will be."

The warmth of his palm. The sincerity in his voice. The way he looked at her, like she was someone worth holding on to, made something flutter deep in her chest.

She nodded, unable to speak.

"You go change," he said gently. "Grace's winter clothes are in the hall closet. Just pull the snowsuit over your outfit. I'll whip us up something to eat. How do you like your eggs?"

"Over medium."

He winked. "Coming right up."

As she turned to go, her fingers tingled from his touch. Her heart thudded, unsteady.

She hadn't felt this seen, or safe, in a long time.

In the bedroom, she found the snowsuit exactly where he'd said it would be. It was deep purple, quilted, and surprisingly lightweight. Grace must've been close to her size, she slipped into it easily. The thought of wearing a dead woman's clothes gave her pause, but Lucas had offered them so matter-of-factly, it didn't feel eerie. It felt... generous.

Before returning to the kitchen, she paused at the mirror. Her hair was a mess, her eyes were still a little puffy, but she didn't look broken anymore.

She looked... alive.

And hopeful.

Something she hadn't felt in days.

Back in the kitchen, the scent of eggs and toast filled the air. Lucas stood at the stove, humming softly to himself, moving with casual ease. He'd changed into dry clothes, another flannel shirt, faded jeans, thick socks.

He looked like a man who belonged in this kitchen. In this life.

She slid into a chair. "You cook, too?"

He shrugged. "When you live alone, it's either cook or starve."

She smiled. "You're full of surprises."

He handed her a plate and sat down across from her. For a few minutes, they ate in silence, sipping coffee and enjoying the quiet.

"You always spend the holidays alone?" she asked softly.

He nodded. "Last year was the first time. This would've been the second."

"That's a shame."

He gave her a slow smile. "Not this year."

Heat bloomed in her cheeks.

They finished eating, and he stood to gather the plates.

"I'll start up the snowmobile," he said. "You'll want boots and gloves. Check the closet for what fits."

She watched him leave, then stared into her empty mug.

Maybe fate hadn't been punishing her when she slid off that road.

Maybe it had been pushing her toward something else.

CHAPTER 8

Olivia clung to the back of Lucas as they made their way down the snow-buried road, her arms wrapped tightly around his waist, her cheek pressed between his shoulder blades.

The world around them was nothing but white.

The snow was so deep that the road had vanished beneath it, erased by the storm. Landmarks she'd noticed on the drive up, fences, signs, trees, were now just vague shapes buried under mounds of powder.

If she were out here alone, she would've had no idea where to go.

The wind sliced across her exposed skin, stealing her breath. Her cheeks were already numb. Lucas had offered her a scarf twice, but she'd stubbornly insisted she'd be fine. She hadn't wanted to admit she was worried, hadn't wanted to look weak.

Now she regretted it. A lot.

She tried to turn her head and take in the wintry land-scape, but the wind was like knives. So instead, she pressed her face into his back, letting the heat from his body warm her skin.

It helped. So did the steady rhythm of his movements and the rumble of the snowmobile beneath them.

At first, Lucas had kept the speed slow, making sure she was comfortable. He even asked her twice if she wanted to turn back. But then he'd sped up, and once she adjusted to the motion, he'd surprised her by doing a quick spin in the snow.

Hanging on to him tightly, she laughed and realized she was having fun. Her heart had shot into her throat, and she'd screamed—but then she'd laughed.

Actually laughed.

It was the first time since the crash that she'd felt anything close to joy.

The wind. The snow. The thrill of movement and freedom.

Lucas laughed with her, glancing back once to check she was still grinning. Then he picked up the pace again.

"You okay?" he shouted over the engine.

"Cold—but good!"

That wasn't a lie. The air temperature was brutal—hovering just below zero, and the wind chill easily dropped it into the negatives. But being close to him, bundled in Grace's snowsuit, she was warmer than she had any right to be.

He'd told her that they couldn't be out long for fear of frostbite.

And despite everything, this felt... good.

Better than good.

Freeing.

The ache in her chest had loosened. The sorrow that had clung to her since yesterday had momentarily faded beneath the sting of the wind and the heat of adventure. It was the first time in days she wasn't thinking about the asshole who'd cheated on her or the job she'd lost.

She was here. In the now. With *Lucas*.

And she was okay.

The wooden gate came into view, its thick horizontal planks partially buried under drifts. She knew they must be close to the highway now. That meant they were also close to the wreckage of her car, her little hatchback that had carried her to work, to dates, to weekend getaways.

And into a snowbank.

She tensed, bracing herself for the sight.

The past 24 hours had upended her life, but she was starting to realize how much worse it could've been. If she'd hit that elk... If Lucas hadn't been behind her... What would have happened to her out in the middle of nowhere with no cell service? And a blizzard howling.

She might've still been trapped out here. Injured. Alone.

Or worse.

A chill ran through her, not from the cold, but from the thought of what *could* have happened.

She buried her face against Lucas again.

Thank God he'd been there.

Thank God he'd stopped.

He slowed the snowmobile to a stop just before the gate and turned off the engine. The sudden silence was startling, just the wind and their breath.

He turned to her. "You all right?"

She nodded, smiling. "Yeah. I'm really enjoying this, actually."

His eyes sparkled. "I'm glad. It's nice to see a smile on your beautiful face."

Her heart skipped.

Beautiful? He thought she was beautiful?

Before she could say anything, her face stung again from the cold, and she winced.

"What did you do with that scarf?" he asked, already reaching into his coat.

"I think I'll take your advice now."

"Good girl," he said with a grin, tugging off a glove and gently cupping her cheek.

His fingers were warm, surprisingly so, and the contrast against her frozen skin made her shiver.

"Your cheeks are getting too cold," he said. "We don't want frostbite."

He pulled a thick wool scarf from inside his jacket and handed it to her. She started to wrap it around her face, but his hands were already there, tugging the ends snugly into place, his gloved fingers adjusting the fabric beneath her chin.

"There," he said softly. "Better?"

She nodded. "Much."

He gave her one last look, something warm and lingering, then climbed off the snowmobile and retrieved the snowshoes from the storage compartment in back.

"I've got to clear the road a bit so we can get the gate open just enough for the snowmobile," he said.

"Let me help."

He shot her a look. "You'll just sink. Stay here where it's safe."

She opened her mouth to argue, but the moment he stepped away, his snowshoes keeping him aloft while the powder swallowed him nearly to the thighs, she realized he was right.

So she waited, watching as he trudged to the gate, dug through the snow until he found the shovel hanging from the fence, and began clearing a path. His movements were strong, steady, efficient.

Fifteen minutes passed. Maybe twenty.

The wind howled. Snow whipped around her. Without Lucas's body heat, the chill began to creep back into her bones.

By the time he returned, he was breathing hard, cheeks flushed, and his coat dusted with snow.

"You ready?" he asked, flashing a grin.

"Freezing," she admitted. "But yes."

He climbed back on, and she wrapped her arms tightly around him, pressing herself close. The heat from his body was immediate and wonderful.

"Good," he murmured. "Get me warm, too."

She laughed softly, resting her cheek between his shoulder blades again. This time, it felt... different.

More intimate.

There was something about holding him like this, trusting him completely in the middle of nowhere, that felt terrifying and thrilling at the same time.

They passed through the now-cleared gate and rode the last few hundred feet to the highway. Her heart clenched at the sight ahead.

Her car.

Or what was left of it.

The little hatchback was almost invisible beneath a thick coating of snow, with only the rear bumper and the side mirror poking out.

She sucked in a sharp breath. "Oh no…"

Lucas cut the engine, and she swung one leg over and jumped off, only to sink past her knees with a startled yelp.

He turned instantly. "Wait! Let me make a path—"

Too late.

Her boots were already full of snow. But she didn't care. She was already moving toward the car, anxiety tightening her chest.

Lucas was beside her in seconds, sliding his snowshoes on and holding out a hand. "Here. Let me go first. Hang onto my coat and stay in my tracks."

She did as he asked, her gloved hands clutching the back of his jacket. Every step was slow and deliberate, the snow crunching beneath his feet as he packed it down for her. Still, she slipped a few times, her boots sinking. Snow crept up her pant legs, and cold began to nip at her ankles.

Finally, they reached the car.

The front end was smashed in, a twisted mess of metal and ice where it had crumpled against the snowbank. The sight made her stomach drop.

"Oh no..."

"It's not as bad as it looks," Lucas said gently. "The snow cushioned a lot of the impact. You're lucky. If you'd hit that elk... this would've been totaled."

He slid his arm around her and pulled her close, offering comfort, warmth, and the solid reassurance of his body.

She leaned into him without hesitation.

"I shouldn't have waited for him," she whispered. "I should've left earlier."

"Don't beat yourself up," he said. "You're here. You're safe. That's all that matters."

She nodded against his shoulder.

"I've got a tote bag," he added. "Let's grab everything important—your suitcase, anything from the glove box."

Together, they worked quickly. She climbed in through the passenger side while Lucas dug around the trunk. Her fingers were stiff, but she managed to gather her charger, her planner, a few gifts she'd packed for her family, and a handful of receipts and registration papers.

They taped her prewritten note to the window, letting

any passing patrol know she was safe and giving Lucas's number.

She took one last look at the car.

It had been her first real purchase after college. A symbol of independence.

Now, it felt like the end of something. And maybe... the beginning of something else.

"I'm lucky I didn't get hurt worse," she murmured.

Lucas looked down at her. "You are. But your life? That can't be totaled, Olivia. You're still standing."

Then, before she could reply, he cupped her face, brushing a bit of snow from her scarf.

And kissed her.

It wasn't tentative.

It wasn't polite.

It was real.

Warm. Deep. Consuming.

Her heart raced as his mouth covered hers, commanding her surrender without force. Her body leaned into his instinctively, her hands clutching his coat as heat poured through her. The kiss tasted like snowflakes and longing, like everything she hadn't known she needed until now.

When he pulled back, his expression was unreadable.

"I want to say I'm sorry," he said. "But I'm not."

She grinned, breathless. "Good. Don't ruin a perfectly amazing kiss."

He smiled, relief flickering in his eyes.

"Come on," he said. "Let's get you back before this storm gets worse again."

He picked up her suitcase and started back. She followed, heart fluttering, tote bag in hand.

She had no idea what was happening between them.

But for the first time in a long time, she didn't feel afraid.

She felt... alive.

CHAPTER 9

What in the hell had made him do that?

He shook off the question as he brushed snow off his boots, trudging into the barn. He could still taste her, her lips, her warmth, the breathy ache of that unexpected kiss.

It had started so innocently this morning. Today, she'd been happier, even laughing on the back of his snowmobile, but when he'd stared down at her sapphire eyes twinkling at him, he'd been unable to resist her mouth.

Her sweet, tasty, full lips had beckoned him, and he'd let his passion overrule his senses, and he'd enjoyed every second of her luscious mouth.

And when he'd kissed her, he'd completely forgotten where they were. It was like he'd been transported to a world where all he wanted to do was linger in her embrace. His cold body had warmed to the point that he'd wanted to push her inside her car and take her right there. But Olivia deserved more. She deserved more, more than a moment, more than heat without meaning, and he wouldn't cheapen what was building between them.

And if that kiss was any indication of the heat simmering between them, he was already in trouble. A good kind of trouble.

In fact, she'd even smiled at him after the kiss when he wanted to apologize. And he'd liked her response, because though he would tell her he was sorry, he really wasn't. Those full lips of hers had haunted him since last night.

Never had he had such an instant attraction to someone.

Her mouth beckoned to him. He'd followed. And when their lips met, the world had narrowed to that single, explosive moment. It wasn't just lust, although lust had a very prominent seat at that meeting. It was chemistry. Something elemental.

He'd forgotten where they were. He'd forgotten the cold. He'd forgotten even himself.

All he'd wanted was to press her into him, to taste every inch of her, to feel that soft curve against his body.

But no.

Olivia deserved more. She deserved respect, not impulse. Affection, not manipulation. The world had already thrown everything at her. He wouldn't add regret to it.

Yet as soon as their lips parted, he wished he hadn't apologized. And he'd liked her response, because though he would tell her he was sorry, he really wasn't. Those full lips of hers had haunted him since last night.

He looked at the snowmobile parked just outside the barn, its tracks buried under silence. He'd dropped Olivia off at the house, along with her things, and then driven to the awning next to the barn.

He needed the cold, needed the silence. Just a few minutes to breathe, to center himself. She'd stirred some-thing deep, left him aroused, aching, and unsure what to do with the fire she'd lit.

Walking to the house, he fought the spitting wind and snow, knowing this storm was not done yet.

When he reached the warm house, he finally exhaled. He unstrapped his snowshoes and left them leaning for later, then shrugged off his snow-sodden coat and hung it near the door. The house smelled like cedar and warmth and the promise of something more. Even after a year alone, he always took a quiet pride in keeping it ready, for Christmas, for memories, for someone.

He could hear her in the narrow kitchen, and there she was, fresh clothes, pink cheeks, even more beautiful than she'd been earlier. This time, the fireplace firelight made her hair catch a glow against the pale walls.

She held a plate of grilled cheese sandwiches. His heart stuttered.

"I hope you don't mind," she said, offering him the plate. "I made us lunch."

He would've knelt. He would've bowed.

"I'm starving," he admitted, voice rough. "Thank you."

She moved close enough to hand him the plate, and he caught the scent of melted cheese and butter, and a trace of lavender from the soap she'd used this morning. That lavender scent clung to him, a gentle echo every time he thought of her.

"Looks good," he said, tasting the cheese and bread, tearing off a chunk.

Sitting down at the table, she took a bite, eyes shining. "Grilled cheese and tomato soup? That'd be perfect today."

He groaned. "We *do* have soup in the pantry."

She gave him a playful look. "I didn't want to rifle through your cabinets without you standing there."

He laughed, then flinched as guilt struck him at the warmth of the moment, realizing how much he wanted to stay right here.

"Search away," he said. "I've got nothing to hide."

She paused, her expression softening. "This house tells me you don't hide much. Your family photos tell me a lot." She touched his shoulder lightly. "In a good way."

He swallowed, that kindness running deep. Talking about his family—, is parents, his sister, the losses, still felt like ripping open old wounds. Better not to rush it.

But she deserved the truth eventually.

He sighed, glancing out the window where snow whipped in sheets. Hours ago, he'd kissed her, but in truth, he wanted to hold her. Forever.

"Your mom wants all of you home for Christmas?" he asked softly.

She nodded. "Usually I skip it when I'm working. But

this time, she insisted. 'Something important.' I thought my boyfriend had talked to her. I thought I was going home engaged."

His gaze broke. "I'm sorry."

She looked everywhere but at him. "Then it all fell apart for the best."

He reached out, brushing a strand of hair behind her ear. His touch burned.

"I'll take you to Whitefish," he whispered.

She looked up, uncertainty and tenderness both. "Would you?"

"Yes," he said without hesitation.

She really needed to get to Whitefish, but she had no way to get there. And the thought of spending another Christmas alone was overwhelming. But he couldn't invite himself to her family Christmas. That wouldn't be right. But he could take her if the weather cleared. If she wanted him to. And he would do whatever she needed. There was no point in someone else's Christmas being ruined.

"Who do you spend Christmas with? It's obvious someone decorated the house."

"I decorate the house," he said. "I do it in my mother's memory. She loved Christmas and it's something I do because I know she would love the fact that her big, burly son is prettying up the house for Christmas."

Oh, how he missed his mother and the rest of his family.

With a sigh, she shook her head. "That's incredible. My father wouldn't even help us decorate the tree when we were kids. But for you to do it in your mother's memory is really touching. And I'm not a grinch, really. I love Christmas, but yesterday didn't go the way I expected."

He took the last bite of his sandwich. It had been good, and he hoped she would cook again for him because his cooking sucked.

"How do I know for certain you're not a grinch?"

A grin spread across her face. "Let's watch a Christmas movie tonight. You choose."

A groan resounded from him and then he grinned. "Terminator. That's my Christmas movie."

Shaking her head, she laughed. "I was going to recommend *Miracle on 34th Street*."

"Not bad, but my Christmas Eve movie is *It's A Wonderful Life*," he said. Watching it had been a family tradition that he just hadn't been able to stop.

"Oh," she said with a sigh, "mine too. Still gets to me every time when the bell rings at the end."

He nodded. "All right, you're not a grinch, and yes, yesterday didn't go as planned. I hope today has been better."

"Much better," she said, standing and taking their dishes to the sink. He watched as she rinsed off the plates and bent over to put them into the dishwasher. She had a perfectly well-rounded ass that had his penis rising to attention. A groan almost escaped his throat.

His thoughts drifted back to last night, when it had been the two of them, alone. The way she'd leaned against the couch, soft and fragile and unmatched with longing suspended in her eyes. He hadn't pressed. He'd held her until she calmed.

This was different. Now she looked... hopeful. Like she'd rediscovered herself.

He reached out, intending only to set his plate down in the dishwasher, but ended up just inches from her. She turned, eyes flicking back to his, recognition and desire both ablaze.

Then he smiled, gently, and before he realized, her lips were on his again.

This time, the kiss was nothing shy or tentative, it was need.

He felt her pressing into him, hand in his hair, her body moving toward him as if every gasp and heartbeat was made for this.

He pressed her back against the sink. His hands slid from her waist to her hips, to the dip of her lower back. They kissed with passion and softness, a dance not of wild lust but of electric longing.

When they broke apart, he was breathless.

"You deserve to be loved and cherished for the woman you are," he said, gasping. He didn't know where that came from, but she turned her large blue eyes on him, and he could see tears shimmering there.

No, he didn't want to make her cry. He wanted to hear her moans of ecstasy. He wanted her to know she deserved to be treated well.

"Olivia," he said with a moan as he dropped to his knees.

His hands ran down her side until he reached her legs and then he spread them. Placing his mouth on her center, he breathed onto her jeans. No, it wasn't exactly what he wanted to do, but it was a start.

She gasped.

"If this is not what you want, tell me to stop," he said.

"No, please keep going," she cried.

He dropped to his knees, heat blooming across his chest as he looked up at her.

She watched him with parted lips and shining eyes.

"I want to show you," he whispered.

His hands slid down her thighs, gently undoing her jeans. Slowly. Reverently. And when he pulled them down, revealing delicate lace beneath, he swallowed thickly.

He pressed his mouth to her, wet and warm, feeding on her scent and softness until she let go, collapsing into pleasure. Her voice rang out, surrendering to him, to her senses.

He reached inside, grounding her, promising care and rhythm. Her wet heat confirmed what he'd felt since the kiss, she *wanted* this.

And he wanted *her.*

His tongue found her, and she came apart around him.

He hovered, catching her soft collapse, pressing his mouth to hers in gratitude and reverence.

When he lifted his head at last, she stared down at him, trembling, breathless.

"You deserve to be treated better," he said, voice deep with longing.

Undoing her jeans, he pulled them down past her knees. She wore a very pretty pair of lacy panties. His fingers found her buttocks and pulled her to his mouth.

"You deserve better than what you've been given. You deserve everything, love, respect, and someone who never takes you for granted.You deserve the best, and I'm going to start by giving you this," he said, unable to say the words that he felt would cheapen this time together.

"Lucas," she cried as his mouth sucked her panties into his mouth right between the junction of her legs. Her hands found their way to his head and she pulled him in closer.

"Yes."

She tasted so sweet, and her juices filled his mouth as her fingers clutched his head and she moaned out loud. So much better to hear her moaning than crying. So much better to give her what she deserved.

His fingers slipped inside her panties and delved into her womanly center. She was so wet for him and that filled him with pride. Oh, she wanted him as much as he desired her.

Pulling her panties down past her knees, he delved his tongue inside her sweet pussy and she cried out. "Lucas, oh goodness."

"Let me give you pleasure," he said, his mouth against her center.

"Oh, yes," she cried.

With his tongue, he circled the lips of her pussy before he gave her clit a little nip. That was all it took for her body to tense, her breathing to stop as she screamed. "Lucas. Oh my, what are you doing to me?"

Then he felt the orgasm overwhelm her as she spasmed around his tongue. He felt her knees buckled as she slumped to the kitchen floor, her jeans and panties still around her ankles. He grabbed her, not letting her fall.

When she reached the ground, his lips closed over hers, and he kissed her thoroughly like he couldn't let her go. When his mouth finally released hers, she stared up at him, and he couldn't stop grinning.

"That's how you're supposed to treat a woman. And you deserve to be treated well."

It was time for her to decide where they went from here. He would never push himself on a woman, but he hoped she would choose him.

Standing, he walked into the living room to give her a few minutes. If she came to him, then he would know she wanted him as much as he desired her. But she had to choose him.

If she didn't, he would be devastated, but he would understand.

It took less than a minute before she came to his side. "I want more."

Thank God. He took her by the hand and led her to his bedroom.

CHAPTER 10

What the hell had he done?

Lucas didn't usually make reckless decisions with women. He was calculated. Cautious. But the moment Olivia's hand had slipped into his, soft and willing, everything inside him had snapped. That kiss outside hadn't just ignited a spark. It had lit a fuse.

And now he was pulling her toward his bedroom with a tension that vibrated between them like a live wire.

She followed him without hesitation, barefoot and flushed from the cold, her eyes wide and filled with something raw, need, maybe. Or trust. He wasn't sure which made his chest tighten more.

When they stepped into his bedroom, she paused. He watched her take it in, the wide king bed, dark wood furniture, flannel sheets, and thick wool blankets. Masculine. Heavy. His. She fit here like she belonged, and that unsettled him more than the weight of desire pressing down his spine.

She looked like she was trying to catch her breath, the soft rise and fall of her chest doing dangerous things to his control. God, she was beautiful. More than that, she was radiant. Her dark hair was slightly wind-tousled, her cheeks pink from the cold. Those blue eyes flicked to him, and something flickered there. Hunger.

And then she moved. She peeled her clothes off piece by piece, jeans first, then her sweater, and finally her bra. Her fingers trembled slightly, but her chin lifted with resolve. She wasn't shy. She was daring herself.

She didn't even seem to notice the breath he sucked in as she crawled into his bed.

Lucas stood there for a second too long, watching her settle beneath the covers, naked, vulnerable, trusting. His throat tightened.

She was here. In his house. In his bed. Because she *wanted* to be.

He shed his shirt quickly, feeling the chill of the air rush across his skin, then undid his jeans and pushed them down with his boxers. His cock sprang free, hard and aching, already painfully aware of what was about to happen. Her gaze fell to him and widened. A quiet sigh escaped her lips, and she bit her bottom one in a way that nearly drove him to his knees.

Still, he paused.

"Olivia," he said, his voice low and thick.

"Lucas…" Her voice wavered just slightly. "I don't do one-night stands."

He crossed to the bed in two steps and lowered himself beside her, catching her gaze. "Honey," he murmured, brushing her cheek with his knuckles, "I'm not a one-night stand."

She didn't look away. Instead, her hand lifted and closed around him, bold and gentle all at once.

A low growl escaped his throat. He clenched his jaw as her fingers explored him with reverent curiosity, like she was learning his shape, committing him to memory. Every soft stroke made his muscles tense.

God, she had no idea what she was doing to him.

"You're not glass," she whispered. "But I want to hold you like you are."

His eyes burned. "You already are, Olivia. You're holding more than you realize."

He pressed his forehead to hers for a second, breathing her in. She smelled like winter and clean linen and woman, warm and soft and everything he hadn't known he needed.

His hand slid along her waist, slowly down her belly, until he reached the heat between her thighs. She sucked in a breath as his fingers brushed across her folds, teasing gently at first, then with more purpose.

She was already wet for him.

The discovery made his pulse hammer. Her body responded to his touch like they'd been lovers in a hundred lifetimes. He parted her slowly, watching her face as he did, the way her lashes fluttered, the way her lips parted on a gasp.

He wanted to memorize every detail of her pleasure.

Her hips arched toward him, and her fingers tightened around his length. He groaned, kissing her throat, then her collarbone, then the swell of her breast. Her skin was like silk, and her moans were the most perfect thing he'd ever heard.

"Lucas," she gasped, her voice trembling.

"Tell me what you need."

"You. Now. Please."

He kissed her lips, slow and deep, then pulled away just long enough to reach into the nightstand. He always kept condoms there, though he hadn't used one in a year. He opened the foil and rolled it on, heart thudding.

Then he settled between her thighs.

The heat of her nearly undid him.

He didn't rush. He met her eyes first, and when she nodded, he pushed forward, slow, steady, savoring the way her body opened to him, wrapped around him, *welcomed* him.

"Jesus, Olivia," he groaned, dropping his forehead to hers. "You feel like heaven."

She gasped, her legs wrapping around his waist. "Don't stop. Please."

He moved inside her in long, slow strokes, letting his body match hers, setting a rhythm that made her moan and cry out beneath him. She clutched at his back, her nails dragging across his shoulders as he thrust deeper, harder, driven by her every sound.

She was incredible.

He'd never felt this kind of connection with anyone. It wasn't just sex, it was something more. Something electric and tender and overwhelming. Like the world had narrowed down to just this, her body, his body, and the wildfire between them.

Her climax built quickly. He could feel it, the way her body tensed, her breath shortened, her muscles tightened around him like a velvet vice.

"I'm gonna—" she gasped, her nails biting into his skin.

"Come for me," he growled, increasing the pressure of his thrusts.

And she did.

Her cry filled the room, her body bucked against his, her orgasm tearing through her like a wave. And the moment she shattered around him, he couldn't hold back any longer.

His own release came fast and hard, crashing over him in a tidal wave of heat and relief. He groaned her name like a prayer and buried himself deep, riding the high until his body gave out and he collapsed beside her.

Silence.

Only the sound of their breathing, shallow, ragged, satisfied.

He pulled her close, their legs tangled beneath the covers, her body soft and warm against his. Her head rested on his chest, and he ran his fingers slowly down her spine, memorizing every curve.

She fit there like she was made for him.

"Are you okay?" he murmured, brushing her hair back from her damp forehead.

She nodded against him. "That was... everything."

"Yeah." He let out a shaky breath. "It was."

They lay like that for a while, letting the warmth settle around them, letting the glow of the moment sink deep into their bones. There was nothing awkward. No tension. Just... contentment.

But Lucas couldn't ignore the way his heart felt like it had cracked wide open.

This wasn't casual. Not for him.

He'd expected a spark, but what he felt was a slow-burning fire he didn't want to put out. He'd known Olivia for less than forty-eight hours, and yet something in his gut told him she wasn't just passing through. She *couldn't* be.

She rolled to her side and looked up at him, smiling softly. "That was incredible, Lucas."

"You're incredible," he said, his voice rough.

Her cheeks flushed pink, and he leaned down to kiss her again, slower this time, more lingering. Their tongues danced together, lazy and warm.

When they finally pulled apart, she nestled close again.

"Promise me something?" she whispered.

"Anything."

"Don't treat this like it didn't mean anything."

He swallowed the lump in his throat and brushed her hair back gently. "Honey, I've never had anything mean *more.*"

She smiled, and he saw the tears glistening in her eyes.

That's when he knew.

He wasn't just falling. He *was gone.*

And for once, he didn't want to stop the fall.

CHAPTER 11

$\mathcal{L}$ucas woke before dawn to the soft tap of sleet and ice against the windowpanes. Snow had its quiet romance, but ice? Ice meant hardened roads, an unforgiving wilderness. His chest tightened at the thought.

Before opening his eyes, though, he inhaled the soft rhythm of her breath beside him. Olivia. Her dark lashes fluttered in her sleep, her hair a soft halo on his pillow. The scent of cedarwood and pear-scented soap mingled with the residual warmth of their closeness. Her shoulder brushed his chest, bare and soft, and Lucas closed his eyes, letting the moment stretch.

He lifted his head and stuffed the blankets aside, heart heavy with emotions as complicated as the weather outside.

He never expected this.

In two days, she had claimed a piece of him that he

wasn't sure would ever be his again, the part that thought love had passed him by.

He swallowed hard, shifting so that he wouldn't wake her. The mattress gave slightly, drawing out a breath from her lips. He paused to listen to the quiet peace inside those breaths, and the muffled wail of the wind outside.

He was falling.

He was terrified.

The sense of having someone to protect, a soul so fragile and yet so full of fire, overwhelmed him. He wanted to shield her from every cruelty: judgmental school boards, dishonest men, broken families. On top of it, he wanted to love her, and that scared him more than any blizzard ever could.

His family... he'd lost them all. His parents and sister were gone, taken by fate and failure to protect them. The aftermath had taught him grief was the great filter: those who cared stayed, those who didn't slipped away.

He smiled into the darkness. He still feared vulnerability, maybe because love had nearly broken him before. But looking at the peaceful face next to him, he knew loving her wasn't beyond him.

He needed to know if he felt for her when he wasn't watching her full lips, the curve of her neck, the way she lay against him. So he eased from the bed, careful not to wake her, and stepped into the chill of the room.

The house was still. The soft hum of the generator, but no heat yet, the thermostat was set low overnight.

He dressed quickly: jeans, flannel, flannel, hat, and gloves. He wanted to watch that warmth return.

Despite the cold, there was warmth ahead.

He padded into the mudroom and strapped on his snowshoes, boots crunching quietly. The cold air stung his lungs, reminding him of reality, chores waited.

Still, he hesitated. The barn. The cattle. Eggs. All things he had to do. Yet each thought pulled him back to her.

Could she be the one?

He forced his steps forward, out the door and into minus ten with the wind howling carving cold across his face. They weren't going to get her car pulled out today. Tomorrow was the day before Christmas Eve and he hoped he could help her get back on the road, and yet, he didn't want her to leave.

He trudged toward the barn, snowshoes muffling the crunch of thick drifts, muscles alert.

Inside, he lit the overhead lamp and found the cart. He worked methodically, stacking hay bales. His shoulders ached, good. The exercise cleared his mind.

But every few minutes, grief and longing tugged through him, bleeding his thoughts back to her.

Would she choose him?

He broke faster than his usual rhythm and he felt the frost-numbed ache of missing her. He stopped, breathless, and closed his eyes.

He scooped one last bale, set it down, and let the tool fall. The cows were fed, the eggs collected, time to get back to Olivia.

With sleet pelting his face, he trudged back to the house. When he opened the back door, he heard her voice.

"Lucas?"

His breath caught cold in his chest, her voice.

"Good morning."

He turned, startled. Olivia stood barefoot in warm flannel pajamas, hair messy but radiant.

The sight broke the spell of the morning's grief and tension. She looked... joyful. Alive. In a way, he'd almost forgotten what was possible.

"Morning," he whispered, and found himself stepping into her.

He bent to kiss her, warm and sudden, that softness he'd awakened to again.

"How did you sleep?" he murmured.

"Like a rock." She leaned against him. "But once you were gone... the bed grew cold."

The truth sent ignition through him.

"We could go back to it."

She laughed, a bright, clear sound. It rang hollowly against everything his heart had been trying to protect.

"You need your strength," she teased.

He nodded, resisting the urge to pull her against him again.

Outside, sleet rattled the roof. There'd be no rescue for her car today. Maybe tomorrow, maybe.

He wrapped his arms around her waist, breath visible in the frosty air of the kitchen.

As he wrapped his arms around her and pulled her up

against him, he couldn't resist sliding his hands up beneath the flannel pajamas she wore.

She jumped and shivered up against him. "You're freezing."

Turning her, he pulled her up against him and lifted her. She wrapped her long legs around his waist.

"Hmm, your bacon is going to burn," she gasped as her lips covered his, devouring him. And he couldn't be happier.

Leaning back, she broke their kiss. "What are we going to do today?"

"Well, we're not going to dig your car out. What if we wear our pajamas all day, stay inside, and play games?" he said, wondering what she would think of the idea of having a pajama day together.

"Oh, what kind of games?"

"Whatever you want to play, darling," he said, holding her tightly against him.

"I love the idea," she said. "Let me finish cooking breakfast and then we'll decide."

When she slid down his front, he all but groaned, his cock rising to attention. Why with Olivia did it seem to have a mind of its own?

Once she stepped back to the stove, he pulled out plates and poured them each a cup of coffee. Suddenly his phone rang and he was shocked that someone had managed to get through.

Beth, she was calling.

Why now?

"I'm calling to invite you to Christmas dinner, if you can get out," she said.

"Well, thank you," he said, knowing he would never accept her invitation. Even if he'd been alone. "But I have plans."

"Oh," she said. "Or are you just being stubborn?"

Yes, he was being very stubborn where she was concerned. She'd walked out of his life and he would never accept her back in. Never.

He walked away so Olivia wouldn't hear him. "No, I'm not being stubborn. I have plans."

No, he didn't. But a thought had been forming in his head about taking Olivia home to her family and meeting her parents. There was so much he wanted with her and the first thing was to meet her family and see their interaction and ask her father for her hand in marriage. Yes, that was quick, but he didn't care. Olivia was who he wanted.

He was certain.

"Look, I made a mistake with you and I was hoping that we could talk things out. My family wanted you to spend Christmas with us. I want you to spend Christmas with me," she said her voice catching.

Was she joking? They would never get back together. It wasn't possible after how she'd left him in his darkest moment. And now Olivia was here and he was falling in love with her.

"It's been a year, Beth," he said. "A terrible year. You left me alone during the worst year of my life."

"You're right," she said. "I just couldn't deal with seeing you grieve so much."

"They were my parents. What did you expect?"

There was a moment of silence. "You're right. I was wrong. I've missed you."

A few days ago, this might have worked on him, but not now. Not with Olivia here. Not with the way he felt about the sweet woman cooking him breakfast. And maybe they wouldn't work out, but something was telling him Olivia was the one for him and he was listening to his intuition.

He ended the call and turned to see her, concern shading her eyes.

"You have a girlfriend and you're cheating on her with me," she said. "I'm going to go pack my bags. I knew this couldn't be this good."

Stunned, he stared as she whirled around and walked out of the kitchen and down the hall.

Damn Beth. Damn her timing. And damn her for making Olivia suspicious. He was not a cheater, and he never would be.

CHAPTER 12

Olivia felt her chest tighten, a familiar ache twisting through her again.

Once more, she'd let herself hope, and once more, she had been buried under the weight of disappointment.

She turned her back to Lucas, shoveled her toiletries into her suitcase as if the act itself could push the pain down, away.

Snow still piled outside their sanctuary, pressing silence against the windows. And yet she felt colder inside than any frozen landscape.

Tears slid down her cheeks, unchecked and sharp. How had this happened again? Just when she thought she'd found something real, something safe…

He walked into the room quietly, and his arms wrapped around her.

She stiffened. No. Not again. She couldn't open her heart only to have it broken again.

He heard her start to close off, but he wasn't going to let her leave, physically or emotionally.

Clarity came in his warm voice. "I'm not cheating on you," he said, tone firm yet gentle. "Beth called me for the first time in a year. Since we broke our engagement."

His words hit her like ice. She turned to face him, wiping tears with the sleeve of her shirt.

"What happened?" she whispered.

He took her hand and guided her into the chair by the window, where the light was soft and forgiving. He drew her onto his lap, and she felt the tension around his mouth, the heaviness in his jaw.

He swallowed and began to speak, slowly, painfully, honestly—

Reaching down, he brushed the tears from her cheeks with his fingers. "Listen to me and you'll understand."

With a sigh, he closed his eyes for a moment and then led her to a chair in the bedroom where he pulled her down into his lap. Gazing at him, she could see the pain etched across his face, the tension in his jaw, the way his brown eyes were dulled with hurt.

This was real. He wasn't lying.

"Thirteen months ago, my parents and my sister were flying back from a dance competition. My sister wanted to become a professional ballet dancer and she'd competed in a competition in Chicago. My father had grown impatient with the airlines and when they landed in Billings, he chartered a small plane to take them to Missoula, and then I was going to pick them up. But they never arrived."

His brown eyes darkened and she could see tears forming in the corners. "The little plane had engine trouble. It appears they tried to turn around, but they didn't make it. All three of them plus the pilot were killed when it crashed in the mountains. It took us three days to find them in the rugged terrain. I was crushed. I'd lost all three of them at once."

Her fingers reached out and caressed his cheek. How did someone deal with three funerals of loved ones at the same time?

"The day after the funeral, Beth decided to end our engagement. During the worst time of my life, she decided to call it quits. So no, I'm not cheating on her or you. That wouldn't be right."

She closed her eyes, holding him. She'd been so quick to suspect betrayal. She was sorry.

She couldn't imagine. Even though she felt jealousy toward her brilliant twin sisters, she would never want them to be killed. The pain would be unbearable for her and her parents. But to lose your entire family in a plane crash.

"Why weren't you with them?"

"The cattle truck was due to pick up the main part of our herd. I told Dad to go with Mom and Sis and I'll stay behind."

Shaking her head, she couldn't imagine the hurt that he'd felt letting his father go in his place.

"He'd not seen my sister dance since she won the high school competition. So I told him I would stay and he could go watch her," he said. "I should have been the one on that plane."

"No," she said, her heart jumping in her chest. "If you had died, then we would not have met."

"No, but my father would be alive," he said.

"But you are their son and will continue their name and your heritage and have children. If you had died, that would all have been lost. I'm sure they would be glad you survived, though it has to be so very tough."

"I just wish they had not taken that small airplane to get home. Dad was trying to get back here to help me, but the cattle had been taken care of. Everything was done."

Stroking his face with her fingers, she reached down and kissed him.

"Beth left me when I needed her the most. There is no way we will ever get back together. You don't have to worry about that."

"I can't lose you, too," he said quietly, the confession raw. "I never cheated. I couldn't."

Tears blurred her vision.

"I'm sorry I didn't trust you. I should have known you would never cheat on me or your previous girlfriend. I let my past cloud my judgment. You're not the big jerk. You're Lucas," she said as she hugged him to her.

"Thank you," he said. "I promise you, I would never ever cheat on you."

Oh, how she wanted to believe that. And already she knew he was a good man. But she'd been burned and she was the one who had to overcome her grief and give him her complete trust. And she wanted to. This man deserved to be loved and trusted and she had to put the past behind her.

"Give me time," she said. "Already you're proving to me what a wonderful man you are."

"Believe me, I'm not like your last boyfriend," he said.

"I know," she said.

The thought of losing everyone she loved in a fatal plane crash was overwhelming. Yes, her family had their issues, but she couldn't imagine them dying that way.

"To lose your family, it must have hurt so much," she said.

"It did," he said and leaned his head against her shoulder. "I've been so lonely. Sure, the servants help around here, but they're not my mother, who was such a loving woman. Or my father, who taught me what I know about the ranch. Or my sister. We teased each other to no end, but she was such a beautiful dancer. I expected to see her with the New York Ballet. She would have been a star."

Olivia put her arms around him and held him tightly. That kind of anguish took a long time to get over.

Putting her mouth to the top of his head, she kissed down his scalp to his forehead, and then she lifted his chin and placed her mouth over his.

Heat spiraled through her as his mouth moved over hers.

Sometimes, the only way to overcome pain was to lose yourself in the arms of another person. That's what she'd done when a high school friend was killed, which was nothing like what Lucas had experienced.

Sliding down his body, she kneeled on the floor, her hands reaching for his belt. Quickly, she unbuckled and unzipped his jeans.

"Olivia," he said, groaning.

"Hush, let me pleasure you," she said, pulling his jeans and his underwear down. He lifted his hips to assist her.

His penis sprang out at her, and she saw the precum glistening on the tip. Leaning over, she wrapped her lips around the head and sucked it into her mouth.

How could a woman desert this man in his darkest hour? How could anyone do that to another human being? Why was it with Lucas, she'd begun to have thoughts of forever with him? She couldn't help but think about raising a couple of kids here in this house. His babies. His children and hers.

Now she understood why he'd been alone. Now she understood why he had no one, and her heart ached for him. How did you get over losing the people you love that way?

Her mouth bobbed up and down on him and her tongue ran around the edge of his cock. She wanted to worship him, make him feel like he was whole again. She wanted to ease his pain and give him only pleasure.

Two nights ago, she'd needed him, but today he needed her. And she wanted to give him the world.

With a moan, she took him deeper into her mouth, and he groaned as he lifted his hips.

"Olivia, baby," he said, and she looked up at him and loved the passion that radiated from his gaze. No longer did grief consume him, and that's what she hoped for.

With her tongue, she traveled the length of his penis, and then she delved down on him once again. His hands gripped her hair.

"I'm going to come," he cried, and that's exactly what she wanted.

While she knew the pain of his family dying was still there, hopefully for a few minutes, she'd given him some happiness. And right now, as much as she didn't want to admit it, she'd give him the world.

A few minutes ago, she'd been afraid that she'd found another loser, but that was her past talking, and all she wanted was to spend as much time as possible with Lucas. Maybe she wasn't ready to say forever, but she was close.

With a groan, he held her head in place as he came inside her mouth, and she sighed with pleasure.

How could she be falling so quickly for this man? A man she would like to spend forever with.

CHAPTER 13

He woke to a soft glow seeping around the curtains, the world outside still hushed under last night's snow. A pale, winter sun hovered on the horizon, stirring the room with fragile hope.

He blinked and tried to move, but the warmth beside him anchored him still.

Olivia, sleep-soft, breath even, lay curled against him. Her hair was a halo of swept strands, her breath rising and falling like the rhythm of calm waves. Every golden ray of morning seemed to pause around her, illuminating the curve of her cheek, the line of her jaw.

Lucas's heart tightened so violently his lungs registered it. This wasn't right. It was *perfect*, but still… too fast. Yet he felt it: she was his.

All of her.

He rolled carefully toward her, eyes scanning her

profile of contentment. He could live in that curve of her collarbone, swallow that soft inhale as she woke.

If she left… it would shatter him.

His fingers traced the soft line of her cheek. His need was more than physical; it quaked through him, love, simple and large, rising like a tide.

But his mind, a past filled with loss, whispered a warning.

Still, he leaned in and brushed her forehead with his lips. She murmured softly, half-lost in sleep.

"Not yet," he whispered.

He eased from the bed and swallowed the bittersweet ache of absence as he tickled his nose with the cold.

The sky was pale and vast, the snow gleaming in dawn's silver light. Ice glazed the window; snow had reached deep into the silence. Everything felt fragile.

Including himself.

The cattle needed feeding. The eggs needed collecting. The road needed plowing. But his heart pounded with one impossible wish: another night with her, whispered promises in the dark, quiet closeness.

He dressed quickly, each layer of wool pressing cold against skin still lingering with her warmth.

Downstairs, he surveyed the blinking heater. The house still held her scent, pine and pear soap, leather, and something faintly wild. He inhaled.

He pulled on his boots, and the familiar crunch of snow delivered him to morning's reality.

He worked methodically, clearing snow, feeding cattle,

and stacking hay. Each motion reminded him of her: the way she'd laughed when he'd joked during breakfast yesterday morning, the way she glanced after him as he left, longing in her eyes. Longing for him.

He tried to hold onto control, pushing down a tremor that wanted to burst free. It had only been two days and two nights, and yet, it felt perfect.

Days ago, he'd been alone. Tomorrow, he would take her home.

Tonight? Tonight, he would try to tell her everything.

Later, the house smelled of frying bacon, faint and delicious, drawing him back to her.

He stepped inside and found her at the stove, hair loosely gathered, cheeks warm with a faint blush.

She turned at his entrance. A smile bloomed that made his chest ache with relief. There were no regrets shadowed on her face. Only happiness seemed to bloom from her eyes.

"You're home," her voice wavered, full of warmth and something like hope.

He closed the distance, pressing a kiss to her temple. "Breakfast?"

She nodded but stopped before serving herself. He swept their plates down to the table.

"I cleared a path to the highway," he said, voice steady. "We can move your car."

She exhaled, mixing relief and fear. "It's not drivable?"

"I don't think so," he admitted.

"Darling, I know that getting home to your family is

important to you," he said. "What if I take you in my truck? It has four-wheel drive."

Glancing up at him, she grinned so big and then jumped up from her chair and ran to him. Her eyes glistened. She rose and pressed against him, arms around his neck, legs winding around his waist.

"Lucas, thank you," she said. "I've been worrying about what to do. You know how important my family is, and missing this Christmas would have broken my heart. I wanted to ask you to go with me and meet my family, but I know you have responsibilities here. What about the cows? You can't go off and leave them."

"I've hired a man to take care of the animals for a couple of days. I'll get you home."

"I don't know how to thank you."

He breathed her in, scent soft in his face. "You don't have to."

Layering her mouth against his, she kissed him deeply as he pulled her onto his lap there at the table. Wrapping her arms around him, she pressed against him.

"You are so good to me."

He was a lucky man. Now if only she would stay with him. Tonight, he was going to tell her his feelings, and he hoped she felt the same way. Whatever she said, he would take her to see her family. But he wanted her forever, not for just this week.

After losing his own family, he knew the importance of being with those you loved during the holidays. No matter what, he would make certain she was with her family.

When she released his lips, he couldn't help but grin at her. "So you no longer fear I'm an ax murderer?"

He grinned, relief, pride, and something deeper flickering like a star in his chest.

She laughed that light carefree way he loved that chased winter shadows from the room.

"No. You're the sweetest man I've ever met."

He drew his brows together. "Sweet? I'd rather be called something manly. Something that makes you swoon."

"Honey, that night when you held me while I cried, you instantly became my hero. You're my big, strong cowboy. You're mine."

Now, that he liked the sound of.

"And you're mine," he whispered.

She stood and commented about getting dressed, and he allowed himself to watch her, warm flannel hugging all the gentle curves he had come to know so well.

He cleared his throat, teetering on the edge of confession.

But he stopped, letting the morning unfold.

She gave a giggle, and he loved to hear her laugh. Since she'd been at his home, she'd gone from the distraught young woman to someone who laughed with ease.

"You'd better let me eat something so we can move your car before a snowplow shoves it further into the snowbank."

Thirty minutes later, they reached her car. It was cold as he jumped out of the truck and went to assess the situation.

"Let me help you," she said.

"You can help me by staying in the truck so I'm not worried about you getting frostbite."

It was going to take a while to dig the car out and then hook it up to his truck.

"But what about you?"

"I'll be taking frequent breaks. Now get in the truck and let's get your car off the road. You stay warm, and when I get cold, you can warm me up."

She grinned at him. "I know how to make you hot."

"Honey, you definitely know how to do that. Now get your sweet little ass back in the truck."

Two hours later, he hooked her little hatchback up to his wench and pulled it to the side of the road leading to his ranch. With the tractor, he'd cleared a path where the tow truck could get to her car.

Next, he called a friend of his who ran a towing service.

"Dan, my girlfriend's car hit a snowbank. It's not drivable, but I moved it to the side of the road leading to my ranch. We're leaving town, but when you get some time, would you pull it to the body shop?"

"I'll take care of it for you," he said. "I can probably get out there tomorrow."

"Great," he told him. "Send me the bill when you get it moved."

As soon as he disconnected the call, she glared at him. "I can pay for it. I'm not your responsibility."

Oh, how he wanted to tell her right then, but he didn't.

He wanted her to be his responsibility. He wanted to take care of her, but that would have to wait.

"You can pay me, but Dan is a good friend, and he'll take care of it properly. And he always gives me a break on the price. That's why I called him."

She licked her lips. "You've been taking care of me for days. I feel that I already owe you for room and board and food and…"

"Don't say sex," he said, laughing. "I'm not your gigolo. And it's been my pleasure to have you here with me."

There was so much he wanted to tell her. Tonight, he would lay his heart on the line and tell her what he desired.

And he wanted it to be permanent.

Tonight, he thought, they would sit by the fire and talk about dreams and families and forever.

Away from the snow, away from fear.

In each other's arms, love dared to grow.

And Lucas vowed: come what may, this Christmas, he would never let her go.

CHAPTER 14

Olivia knew she *should* be happy. Lucas had arranged for her car to be towed to the shop, offered to take her home in the morning, and treated her with more care than any man ever had.

And yet... something in her resisted. It wasn't him. It was her.

No man had ever stepped in to handle things like this before, not without expecting something in return. Every time Lucas did something generous, part of her tensed. Part of her waited for the other shoe to drop.

She heard him call her *his girlfriend* earlier, and it sent a rush of heat through her chest, half joy, half panic. She wanted to be his. God, did she want to be his. But she'd never known how to *trust* that someone would stay. That someone could love her and mean it.

The truth was ugly and hard to admit: the problem with her past relationships hadn't just been *them*.

It had been *her choices*.

Her fear disguised as confidence. Her pattern of picking emotionally unavailable men and pretending it didn't hurt when they pulled away.

But Lucas… Lucas was everything she claimed she wanted. Steady. Strong. Protective. Kind. He looked at her like she was a miracle, not a burden.

And still, she was afraid.

Would she have chosen him if fate hadn't intervened? If that elk hadn't stepped in front of her car on a snow-covered Montana road? Probably not.

Even though the man was so damn handsome that her breath caught in her throat when she gazed at him. He was sweet and kind, and she'd been stupid about the types of men she'd chosen.

But at this moment, she chose him. She wanted him and no one else. Never had a man treated her as well as he did. Never had a man made certain she was happy. Never had a man made love to her like he did.

Tonight, her last night at the ranch, he'd fixed a lovely dinner. They had worked side by side in the kitchen, creating a meal that was better than restaurant quality. They had laughed and kissed and tasted and tempted one another all night, but would it be like this forever?

It had felt easy. *Real.* And that scared her more than anything.

She had a lousy track record, and what if tomorrow she woke up and Lucas was a complete asshole? What if he wasn't like what he seemed here at the ranch, and she'd given her heart to him?

She'd be devastated.

But here they were, four days later, and something deep inside her knew: *he was it.*

She sat beside him on the living room floor, a thick blanket beneath them, the fire crackling beside them, and champagne flutes in their hands. He'd taken the couch cushions and laid them down by the hearth like a makeshift bed, cozy and intimate. The only light came from the flames licking the logs and a few candles flickering nearby.

"Why champagne?" she asked, tipping her glass slightly.

Lucas's gaze locked on hers, firelight catching the gold in his eyes. "Because tonight, I wanted to celebrate. Meeting you. Having these days with you."

He touched his glass to hers gently. "To you, Olivia. You're the best thing that's happened to me in years. I've never met a woman that I've instantly fallen in love with. It was like the universe dropped you into my world out of nowhere. And I love you with all my heart. You've changed my life."

The words struck her heart like a bell. Clear. Resonant. Irrevocable.

She blinked, speechless.

"I've never met a woman I fell for this fast," he said. "But the moment I pulled you out of that snowbank, I knew. It wasn't just a rescue. It was *right.*"

She raised her glass slowly and clinked it to his. "Lucas… I thought I was going to get *engaged* this weekend." Her voice cracked. "But now I see that wasn't love. This—" she gestured between them "—this feels different. But what if I'm bad at choosing men? What if I ruin this too?"

He smiled, setting down his glass. "Maybe you didn't choose me. Maybe the universe chose *me* for *you.*"

That was an interesting perspective. She'd never considered that before.

She tilted her head. "You really believe that?"

He nodded. "What are the odds I was behind you on that road? That the elk ran out *right then*? That I was the one to pull you out of that ditch, bring you home?"

He looked around the room, eyes distant but full. "My parents had a rare kind of love. They laughed more than they fought. They held hands even when no one was looking. That's the kind of life I want. The kind where you're partners through everything. Where love is the *foundation,* not just the spark."

He turned to her fully now. "I want that with you, Olivia. I know we haven't had much time, but I know what I feel. And I want a future with you."

Her heart thundered. "You're serious?"

He nodded. "I'm *dead* serious. I want to marry you. Build a life. Have kids. Wake up next to you for the next fifty years. All of it."

Tears stung her eyes. "I love you too," she whispered, voice cracking. "But I'm scared, Lucas. I've been wrong before. I've *hurt* before. And I don't know how to stop doubting myself."

He reached for her hand and laced their fingers together. "Then let me carry the doubts for both of us. I'll love you through them. I'll prove to you every day that I'm not going anywhere."

Her breath hitched. "You really want all of that… with *me*?"

"I want it with *only* you. Fate brought us together, but love will bind us forever."

She paused, staring into his eyes, her heart thumping like it was a racehorse. "Okay. Let's go slow. One day at a time."

A grin tugged at the corners of his mouth. "So… we wait until *next week* to get married?"

She laughed, shoving him lightly. "You're impossible."

"I'd marry you tomorrow," he said seriously. "But I'll wait. I'll wait as long as you need. And every day I'll show you that what we have is special."

Emotion swelled inside her. This man, this unexpected, rugged cowboy, had cracked open something inside her that she hadn't even known was still beating.

She leaned in and kissed him. Softly at first. Then deeper. Longer.

And suddenly, they weren't two people in front of a fire anymore. They were something else entirely.

His arms wrapped around her as he lowered her gently onto the cushions. Their champagne glasses were forgotten. Their doubts suspended.

Now I'm going to make love to you, right here in front of this fire. I'm going to have you screaming my name."

A giggle escaped her. "What if I have you screaming?"

"Darling, that wouldn't be hard," he said as he leaned down and kissed the side of her neck, sending a shiver through her.

His touch was reverent. Slow. She felt worshipped. Wanted. Loved.

He whispered her name like it was sacred. And every kiss felt like a promise.

Was she doing the right thing? Was Lucas the man for her? She believed so, but only time would tell. Of one thing she was certain, he'd claimed her heart. She loved him deeply, and that was why committing herself to him was so frightening.

She took a deep breath, his musky scent causing her pulse to accelerate. How could just the smell make her body react with such desire? The touch of his flesh against hers filled her with heat.

Staring into his eyes, she felt like he had grabbed her heart and refused to let go. And she was glad because she wanted him so badly.

His lips covered hers, and she melded into him, loving the feel of his strong muscles surrounding her. Her arms wound around his neck, pulling him closer, needing to feel more of him.

While their tongues danced, a moan resounded from her, and she pulled his body tightly against her own. Just a touch and she could feel her body responding to him. Just his smell had her whimpering with need for him. Just a kiss had her needing him deep inside her.

Releasing her mouth, he gazed into her eyes. A shiver passed through her at the desire that radiated from his stare. She wanted him as much, if not more, than the passion she saw reflected in his eyes.

"You're mine. And I want more than just four days. I want a lifetime," he said, his mouth covering hers as she gave herself to him. This time, she hoped and prayed he was forever.

His kiss became more savage than gentle as he let her know she was his and he claimed her as his own, and she reveled under the assault of his lips. This was what she wanted.

This strong man would protect her, love her, and give her the life she'd dreamed of for so long. This man had become her everything, and she couldn't imagine leaving him. Not for a day or a week. She wanted him beside her.

Maybe he was right that the universe had sent her exactly what she'd been searching for and unable to find on her own – a respectable man who would love her until the day she died.

His tongue entered her mouth, sweeping the inside of her lips, leaving her gasping and needy. She pressed her body against his, seeking his hardened flesh between her thighs, yearning only to satiate the desire Lucas created.

How she wanted him—hard and filling the empty holes in her soul, the places only Lucas could fill.

Why did it feel like this was where she belonged, where

she was meant to be? The storm had brought them together, and tomorrow, they would face the world. A united couple with dreams of a life together. Dreams of a wedding, a home, and a family.

His hungry lips coaxed her, pervading her body with delight until she no longer heard the voices whispering inside her head that he would cheat on her just like all the others. Pushing those thoughts away, she reminded herself this was Lucas. The man who'd rescued her, taken care of her, and promised her a lifelong love.

And she knew he would do exactly what he promised – love her until the day she left this earth. Could she give him the same?

Their lips came apart, though their breaths continued to commingle in the firelight.

"You have too many clothes on," she said with a gasp. "I want you naked and deep inside me."

A smile curved his lips. "Your wish is my command."

Rising above her, he removed his shirt while she fumbled with the sweater she wore. Undoing his belt, he unhooked his jeans and slid the zipper down before he kicked off his house shoes. Then he was reaching for her jeans, and she sighed as he unhooked the button and slid them down her legs. She unclasped her bra, throwing it to the side.

"Olivia, I need you so bad," he whispered.

She shuddered at the sound of his voice, needy with desire, thrilling her. His lips continued their path down her neck to the top of her shoulder, his tongue lingering on the sensitive curve of her nape. His lips and warm breath sent shudders rippling through her.

Only with Lucas had she been so responsive, so filled with love. So needy for his touch.

He raised his head and gazed into her eyes, his expression scorching her with its intensity. She watched as he lowered his mouth toward her. Eagerly, she rose to meet him.

Slanting his lips across her mouth, he kissed her deeply and thoroughly as if to mark her as his own.

Lucas was exactly who and what she'd been searching for. And this man not only made her body sing with delight, but he filled her soul and made her feel whole again. He was the real deal.

Greedily, he placed his lips on her breast, his tongue lavishing attention on her nipple. She arched her back, giving him more access to her breast, her hands clutching the hair on top of his head. His body molded to the contours of her skin, and she delighted in the feel of his muscular thighs and hard chest, firm and solid against her. For every place their skin touched, she rejoiced in the way his flesh warmed her with a heat that burned from within.

A log in the fireplace rolled, sending a shower of sparks up the chimney, but sparks danced between them. Sparks that burst into flames when they touched.

His hand skimmed down her rib cage, over her stomach, and lower until he touched the silky folds between her legs. Searching and finding her very center, he delved his fingers into her hot, moist core.

Olivia gripped the blanket he'd placed on the floor, clutching the material in her fists. Never had she experienced the frenzied passion Lucas incited within her.

Never had she gazed into a man's eyes and known they would be together forever. In the firelight, she stared at him as she cried out, disintegrating beneath his hand, quivering with her release, knowing that only with him did she come so fast and so hard.

She lay spent, her heart racing, her breathing jagged as she clung to Lucas, his broad shoulders hovering above her.

"Lucas," she gasped. "Please."

He kissed her temple, her eyelids, and her nose. She felt him rigid and hard against her leg, waiting patiently for her to catch her breath. Lucas made her feel like a loved woman, sheltered and protected.

"Darling, I need to be inside you, now," he said, his voice tense. "I need you to brand your name on my heart."

She whimpered at his words, the thought of his desire astonishing.

Reaching down, she located the proof of his longing between his legs. She touched him, wrapped her fingers around his shaft, and lovingly stroked him before she moved him between her legs.

"I need you too, Lucas," she gasped. "Inside me, now."

They didn't take the time to grab a condom, but she didn't care. Yes, it was reckless, but at this moment, her heart knew he was the one.

She gazed into his passion-filled eyes, his face a grimace of pleasure and pain.

The feel of him, hot and smooth, was intoxicating; she felt his blood pulsating through him.

With her free hand, she cupped his chin and pulled his mouth down to hers.

How she needed him. How she wanted him. And the pure joy she felt at that thought thrilled her.

His lips caressed hers, teasing and sweeping into her mouth with an urgency that gripped her, holding her captive with his kiss. She shifted to accommodate him, lifting her hips to meet him as she arched her back, her hips rotating slightly to give him deeper access to her center.

He plunged into her, and she welcomed him, the pleasure filling her.

With every driving stroke, she matched him, met him. She felt her heart mate with his, knowing he would be hers forever.

Passion burst forth like a shower of sparks, scorching her with its intensity as he rhythmically pushed her toward the flame.

"Lucas," she screamed as she tumbled, end over end, over a cliff until she landed fractured and shattered in his arms.

With a shuddered cry, he reached his own release, and together they lay helpless, sweating, and completely undone.

"I'll love you until my last breath," he whispered. "You and only you."

Her heart was filled to near bursting at the feelings he evoked. This time, she thought she'd chosen wisely. This time was right.

"I love you, Lucas," she whispered, tears filling her eyes.

At long last, she'd found happiness. At long last, she'd found the one.

CHAPTER 15

Olivia zipped the final pocket of her suitcase and stood still, her hand resting on the handle. The guest room, where she had only spent one night, felt almost sacred now. A room that had once held her when she was broken, aching, and lost, now bore the faint imprint of a woman transformed.

She wasn't the same girl who'd stumbled through Lucas's front door, soaked and stranded and utterly heartbroken. She was still healing, still afraid… but this morning, her heart was full. Full of something she hadn't dared hope for in years.

Love.

She wheeled the suitcase out to the living room and smiled as Lucas looked up. "I'm all packed," she said softly.

He gave a tight nod, but there was a weight behind his eyes. She could feel it even across the room.

"Good," he replied, his voice low and unreadable.

The mood shifted. The air between them thickened with unspoken tension. Olivia studied him. His broad shoulders were stiff, his jaw tight. He was trying to hide something. Not from her, but maybe from himself.

She knew that look. That hesitance. That quiet ache.

He didn't want her to leave the ranch.

And if she was honest, part of her didn't want to go either.

"I know I'll be back," she said, walking toward him. "But this time… this house… you… It's been everything I didn't know I needed. I came here scared, wounded, certain I'd lost everything. But I didn't. I found something better. I found you."

She rose up on her toes and kissed him gently, sweetly. The moment their lips met, some of the weight seemed to slip off his shoulders.

"Thank you," she whispered against his mouth.

His hand wrapped around hers, anchoring her.

"Thank you," he murmured, his voice hoarse. "I'm a little nervous about meeting your family."

She smiled. "My mother's going to adore you. My dad's going to love talking ranch life with you, especially if you like football and gardening. He has a whole little 'ranchette' setup in the backyard. Chickens and everything."

Lucas chuckled, but the warmth in his laughter didn't fully reach his eyes. Not yet.

She tilted her head. "What's wrong?"

He didn't answer right away. Instead, he turned to glance around the room, at the garlands, the holly-lined shelves, the dimmed glow of the tree in the corner. It was quiet now. Still. The kind of quiet that came before the pain of memory.

"I just wish… I wish you could've met my family," he said finally. "My mom… you two would've loved each other. And Grace? My sister would've been your biggest cheerleader. My dad… he would've said I finally got it right."

She walked to him slowly and melted into his arms. He held her tightly, burying his face in her hair as they stood in the silence of Christmas, wrapped in garland and grief.

"They're here," she said softly, her lips against his collar. "I feel them. In the way this house wraps around us. In the way you love me, with such quiet strength. I know they'd be proud of you. Proud of us."

She pulled back and gave him a small, brave smile. "I think we should name our first child after one of them."

His breath hitched, and he stared at her with so much love that it made her chest ache.

"That would mean the world to me," he said. "And… I've been thinking. I want to put together a video of them. All the old photos, the movies we took every Christmas. You know, those old VHS recordings that no one ever watches again."

Her lips twitched. "So you want to be that dad."

"What dad?" he teased.

"The one who pulls out the home movies every Christmas Eve while the kids groan and roll their eyes."

He laughed and kissed her temple. "Exactly that, Dad. I

want them to know who their grandparents were. To remember them, even if they never met them. I want their legacy to mean something."

Tears welled in her eyes, unbidden. "You're really serious about us."

"I am," he said. "I know I've asked you to marry me… but every time I picture the future, I only see it with you in it. I want a life with you. A home. Kids. Laughter. Ordinary things that feel like miracles."

She swallowed. Her hands trembled slightly as she clasped his.

"Be patient with me, Lucas. I know I love you. I know this feels right. But sometimes I wake up thinking this has all been a dream… and I'll go back to the girl in the broken-down car with nothing left."

He framed her face in his palms and looked at her like she was made of stars.

"No dream," he said. "You and me. Forever. And I'm going to talk to your dad this weekend. I want to do this right."

She grinned through tears. "Oh, Daddy is going to be so shocked."

He kissed her quickly, then pulled back to glance at the clock. "We should get going if we want to make it before dark. Have you talked to your mom yet?"

She shook her head. "Still no signal. I figured I'd wait until we're closer and just surprise her."

"Let's go then," he said, taking one last look around the house.

"Merry Christmas, Mom. Dad. Grace," he said, his voice catching. "I hope you're celebrating in Heaven."

He walked to the Christmas tree and flicked the lights off.

But just as the room dimmed, one tiny light sparkled through the shadows.

A single ornament, his mother's favorite, spun slowly on its hook, twinkling softly in the morning light.

He stared at it, his throat tightening.

"Thanks, Mom," he whispered.

Outside, the wind was gentle, the snow crisp underfoot as he helped Olivia into the truck. She watched him glance back at the house one final time.

For the first time in over a year, Lucas wasn't spending Christmas alone.

And for the first time in her life, Olivia believed she might actually have found a home in someone's heart.

Not just for the season.

But for always.

CHAPTER 16

The closer they got to Whitefish, the faster Olivia's heart raced—not from nerves, but from excitement. Just five days ago, she had been driving this same stretch of road alone, watching the sun vanish behind snow-drenched mountains and hoping to make it home before dark. Five days ago, she thought she was heading toward an engagement that would finally make sense of a complicated, unfulfilling relationship.

And then the snowstorm came. And everything changed.

She reached across the truck's console, brushing her fingers against Lucas's. He smiled at her, his warm brown eyes shining with the same anticipation she felt curling in her chest.

"I can't believe I'm bringing you home," she said, her voice soft with wonder. "But I also… can't believe I ever planned to arrive here with anyone else."

Lucas glanced at her, his smile tilting with affection. "Fate had other plans."

God, he was beautiful. Not just physically, though his strong jawline and sun-warmed skin made her stomach flutter, but in his soul. He was kind. Steady. Gentle in all the ways her heart had secretly begged for.

She couldn't wait for her family to meet him. Her real family—the people who knew her better than anyone else in the world. Surely, they would see what she saw in him.

As they turned into her parents' long, winding drive, Olivia felt her heart skip a beat. Cars already lined the front of the house, parked beneath the arched pine trees heavy with snow. Twinkling lights adorned the porch, and the windows flickered with warmth and movement.

"Everyone's here," she murmured.

Lucas parked the truck and gave her hand a squeeze. "Ready?"

"They're going to love you," she said, beaming. "Just like I do."

He leaned over and gave her a quick kiss. "Let's go meet the family."

He climbed out first and walked around to open her door, ever the gentleman. Just as Olivia stepped out and adjusted her coat, the front door swung open.

And the moment shattered.

There, standing on the porch like some grotesque reminder of everything she was trying to leave behind, was *him*.

Steve.

The big jerk.

Of course he would show up like nothing had happened, with that familiar smirk and an entitled gleam in his eyes.

"About time you got here," Steve said, as if he'd been waiting for her. As if they were still something.

Olivia stopped cold.

"No," she said under her breath. "Oh no. No."

Lucas immediately turned toward her. "What's wrong?"

"That's my ex," she said tightly. "*Steve.*"

Lucas's jaw tensed.

And then, as if things couldn't get worse, Steve sauntered off the porch like a golden retriever greeting someone he'd abandoned hours earlier.

"Darling," he said, as if they were lovers on a break, "I flew in this morning to surprise your family. Thought I'd come early, get to know them a little better. Who's this?"

He gestured vaguely toward Lucas.

Lucas didn't offer a handshake. "Lucas Peterson."

The name was simple. Solid. Said with calm, quiet authority.

Olivia stepped in front of Lucas like a shield. "You have *so* much nerve showing up here."

Steve looked surprised. "What are you talking about?"

"You *remember* where I found you, don't you?" Her voice shook, more from the adrenaline than anything else. "You remember who was in your bed?"

He shrugged, unapologetic. "I was drunk. She meant nothing to me."

"Oh, how original," she snapped. "You know what *means* something? Respect. Trust. You threw all of that away."

"I came here to win you back."

"Well, you wasted your time." Olivia took Lucas's hand and stepped closer to him, drawing strength from the man beside her. "This is the man who picked me up out of the snow when your betrayal nearly got me killed. He's the man who took me in, cared for me, loved me. *Because of you*, I could've frozen to death. But instead, fate intervened, and I found someone worthy."

She took a breath. "You think showing up now is romantic? It's pathetic. You had your chance. You blew it. You're not welcome here. In fact, we'll send you a wedding invite… as a courtesy."

Steve's jaw dropped. "You *cheated* on me?"

"No," she said coolly. "We were over the moment I saw you with Cynthia. You just didn't know it yet. Go pack your bags, call yourself an Uber, and get off my parents' lawn."

He stepped toward her, but Lucas gently pulled her behind him, calm but firm. "She's made her choice. I suggest you respect it."

There was something unmistakably final in Lucas's voice.

Steve stood frozen for a second, then turned and stalked back inside.

Olivia exhaled and turned toward the porch, where her *real* family had been watching the entire exchange.

Her parents looked stunned but relieved.

"Mom. Dad," Olivia said, her heart suddenly lighter than it had been in days, "this is my fiancé, Lucas Peterson."

Her father blinked once, then burst into a wide grin. "*Thank God* it wasn't that boy toy."

Olivia laughed, the tension shattering in her chest. "Dad! How do you even know what a boy toy is?"

Her mother giggled, stepping forward to wrap Lucas in a warm hug. "We are *so* happy to have you here."

Lucas smiled, humbled. "Thank you, ma'am."

Her father shook Lucas's hand, squeezing it tight. "Welcome to the family, son."

Emotion caught in Olivia's throat as she hugged them both.

"Mom, I was so scared," she whispered. "Lucas found me when I was stranded. He took me in. He… he saved me in every way."

Her mother stepped back and looked at her with glistening eyes. "I think you've found your forever man."

"I *know* I have," Olivia said, reaching for Lucas's hand again. "And there's not a single doubt left in my heart."

Lucas pulled her close and kissed her temple. "You were amazing, baby. I'm proud of you."

They walked into the house together, the warmth and love inside making her feel at home instantly. The Christmas tree sparkled in the corner, garland draped across the fireplace. Holiday music played softly from the living room.

It felt like magic.

"Where's everyone else?" Olivia asked.

Her dad sighed. "This weather. Emma's stuck in an airport. Amelia… well, apparently she's snowed in somewhere with a paramedic. Don't ask. But *we're* just grateful Lucas got to you when he did."

She squeezed Lucas's hand. "So am I."

Then something clicked.

"Wait… what was the big *urgency* that you needed us all home this Christmas?"

Her mom exchanged a look with her father, then gave Olivia a coy smile. "Besides wanting all of our children together for the holidays? We do have an announcement."

Her pulse jumped. "Is it… health-related?"

"No, sweetheart. Nothing bad," her mom said. "In fact, it's wonderful. But we want to wait until your sisters get here before we share."

Olivia narrowed her eyes, curious. "You're not pregnant, are you?"

Her mom burst out laughing. "Oh heavens no. Let's just say… it's a happy surprise."

That did nothing to ease Olivia's curiosity.

"Well," her mother said, changing the subject with a twinkle in her eye, "why don't you and Lucas sit and tell us how you met?"

She looked at him, then back at her parents, her heart threatening to burst.

"It's kind of a crazy story," she began. "But in the middle of the worst snowstorm in years, when everything in my life was falling apart… the universe gave me Lucas."

Her mother's eyes softened. "Sounds like fate."

"It was," Olivia said. "And now, I think we're going to need to start planning a wedding. Sooner rather than later."

Lucas's arm wrapped around her waist, grounding her.

"Or right now," he whispered.

She turned to him, laughing as tears welled in her eyes. She had come here uncertain. Scared. Fragile.

But now, she stood strong beside the man who'd put her back together.

She was home.

And she was loved.

Forever.

CHAPTER 17

*E*mma Miller hated flying.

Actually, *despised* was a more accurate word. Hurtling through the sky in a metal tube with recycled air, lukewarm coffee, and zero legroom? Yeah, she could live a hundred years without it and be just fine.

But flying into small regional airports like *Missoula, Montana*? That was next-level torture. Especially in winter. Especially when connecting flights were few, the weather was unpredictable, and you had better odds of riding a reindeer to your final destination.

She crossed her legs in the plastic chair by the gate and stared at the growing storm through the floor-to-ceiling windows. Thick, dark clouds gathered above the mountains like a threat whispered by nature itself.

Not good.

The sign still flashed "Delayed," mocking her with its stubborn glow. But for how long? Another hour? All night?

Dread coiled in her stomach, any longer and she'd be sleeping in this freezing terminal with nothing but a vending machine dinner and fluorescent lights buzzing overhead.

Already, she could see a line forming at the rental car counter. Her heart sank. Were they all about to be stranded here? Were they beating her to a car?

She pulled out her phone and tapped through the local weather updates.

Blizzard Warning in Effect

Whitefish expected to receive 5–6 feet of snow in the next 48 hours.

"What the hell am I even doing here?" she muttered to herself.

It wasn't like she looked forward to the family Christmas. Not anymore. Not with Olivia, who seemed to constantly be in crisis. Or Amelia, her practically perfect twin sister with her golden glow and unflappable charm.

Meanwhile, she was the "smart one." The "responsible one." The overachiever who paid her own rent, filed her taxes early, and quietly climbed the ladder at her company while no one really asked what ladder it was.

She could become the President of the United States, and her parents would probably ask if she was getting enough sleep.

So, what exactly do you do again, Emma?

She rolled her eyes at the memory, staring just in time to watch a sleek private jet land effortlessly on the runway. A Learjet. Of course. Probably someone flying in from

Aspen or Vail for a weekend of skiing and cocoa served by staff in matching Patagonia jackets.

Must be nice.

Like a voice from the heavens, the announcement echoed through the terminal, not with salvation, but with the weight of a funeral dirge, heavy and foreboding.

"We regret to inform you that all flights out of Missoula have been canceled due to the incoming storm. Please check with a gate agent. Baggage will be returned to carousel three."

There it was. Her worst travel nightmare coming true.

Stranded.

She shot to her feet and immediately dialed hotels nearby, cradling her phone between her shoulder and cheek while she opened her travel app.

"No availability."

"We're full, ma'am."

"You might try the Gilded Palace out by the truck stop."

Oh, hell no.

She'd driven past that place once. It looked like the set of a B-grade horror movie, or worse, a hotbed of bacteria and bad decisions.

With a groan, she plopped back into her seat. *Could she even sleep here at the airport?*

There was no way she was braving the Gilded Petri Dish.

Her eyes darted toward the rental car counter again. The line had thinned. Maybe there was still a shot.

Worth a try.

Snatching her purse, she practically jogged to the counter. "I'll take whatever car you've got. I don't care if it's a scooter with snow tires."

The woman behind the counter blinked, clearly exhausted from dealing with angry travelers. "We have a 2018 Toyota Camry. High mileage but solid."

"I'll take it—"

"I was here first."

A male voice spoke from just behind her, deep, smooth, and unmistakably annoyed. And familiar.

She stiffened. Could he not see her?

"I'm literally standing at the counter."

"Yeah, and I was walking up to it before you cut in line."

"I didn't cut. I claimed."

The man had been walking while texting. It wasn't her problem, he had moved too slow.

The clerk held up her hands. "Too late. Just rented it to a seventy-year-old woman who looked like she could throw down. I'm out of cars."

Emma groaned. *Perfect.* No hotel. No flight. No rental car. This was shaping up to be the most festive holiday ever.

And then she heard it. That voice again.

Softened this time. Almost… surprised.

"Emma?"

She turned.

And the moment stretched.

Emerald green eyes blinked at her. A face she hadn't

seen in more than a decade, but one she recognized immediately.

Holy. Hell.

Theo White.

Her brain stuttered. *Theodore White.* The kid who used to sit two rows behind her in AP Calculus. The quiet genius who created a video game during lunch period. The boy with thick glasses, no fashion sense, and the social skills of a bookshelf.

Except… that boy was long gone. And this man had all her erogenous zones firing on high alert. What the hell was he doing in the airport in Missoula?

White Christmas

White
Christmas
Come Home for Christmas
USA TODAY BESTSELLING AUTHOR
SYLVIA MCDANIEL

JOSHUA

Joshua Burnett liked women. Lots of women. And dating more than one at a time was never out of the question. The more the merrier. Date them, bed them, and then tell them good-bye. That was his motto and he lived by it religiously.

He rolled over in bed next to his latest conquest, Marcy Anderson. They'd been sleeping together for the last month, and he liked how it was all about the sex. No commitments, no promises of forever, nothing but a good time. And Marcy was the one who set the rules, not him.

But they fit very well within his own set of regulations.

Lying in bed, he glanced at her. "We're still going to the rodeo tonight?"

"Yes," she said, rising from the bed naked.

He liked her body, and he liked the way she enjoyed partying late into the night, having sex until dawn, sleeping until noon, and then afternoon sex. Every weekend, they stayed at either his place or hers.

She'd let him know right up front that she wasn't interested in marriage or anything permanent and that was all he needed to hear. When the time came and he was finished with her, he'd say good-bye.

"Guess we better get up and get ready to go," he said, throwing his feet over the side of the bed. It was the Friday after Thanksgiving and instead of fighting crowds at the mall, they had spent the day in bed.

He jumped into the shower and she joined him there.

"We're invited to go out with the bull riders after the rodeo," she said, washing his back.

"Sounds like fun," he said, thinking how those men lived life on the edge and partied like it was their last night.

And it could be.

After stepping out of the shower, he pulled on a fresh pair of jeans, tucked one of his good shirts into his pants, and slipped on his boots.

Turning, he watched Marcy spray her hair, making certain the curls stayed in place. Her makeup was spotless and he knew he'd be the envy of every cowboy at the rodeo tonight.

She turned and smiled.

"Ready?"

"Yes," he said. They started toward the garage. The sound of knocking on his front door had him frowning.

"Let me get that and then we'll go." It was probably one of the workers there to tell him something about the cattle.

After walking into his living area, he opened the front door, and his eyes widened.

An old girlfriend from over a year ago, Skylar Beal, stood in front of him, looking gorgeous, her blonde hair longer than ever, holding a baby.

"Skylar," he said, surprised. She hardly seemed like the motherly type. "What are you doing here?"

She thrust the baby into his arms and he had no choice but to accept the child or let it drop to the ground.

"What the hell?"

Her brown eyes flashed with determination and she stepped back far enough away he couldn't give her the baby back.

"It's your turn. I haven't gone out and had fun in ages, Josh. I've been pregnant then dealing with Mia. Now it's my turn for some fun. You can watch her for the weekend."

The woman had completely lost it. "I'm not watching your kid. Why would I?"

The smirk he had hated from the day he met her filled her face. "She's yours, hotshot. Deal with it. I had to."

Terror filled his chest and his heart raced like a formula one driver's car nearing the concrete wall.

"What? This baby isn't mine," he yelled.

Two big sapphire eyes popped open and the baby's bottom lip trembled before she belted out a cry.

"Now you've done it," Skylar said, dropping a bag on the ground at his feet. "Her formula, diapers, everything you'll need is here in this bag. I'll be back late Sunday to pick her up. Have a great weekend getting to know your daughter Mia."

Turning around in her cowboy boots, she all but ran

down the stairs and jumped into her Corvette. The engine roared to life and she backed out of his drive, spinning gravel as she took off.

Shocked, he stared down at the baby in his arms. This child was his? No…

What the hell was he going to do? He didn't know anything about taking care of babies. What kind of mother just ran off and left her child with an amateur?

Marcy came up behind him. "Are you ready?" Her eyes widened with concern. "Where did the baby come from?"

"Skylar just dropped her off. Said she was mine." He wasn't certain he believed her, but what was he going to do? Her mother was gone.

The baby cried louder, and with disbelief, Joshua picked up the diaper bag, brought it into the house, and closed the door.

Marcy shook her head. "Ew. I don't do screaming babies or men with kids. It's been fun, Josh. Call me if you get this straightened out. But not if you have a kid. Have a good night. I'm going to the rodeo."

He could only watch as she picked up her purse and overnight bag and walked out the door. And just like that, she was out of his life. Probably forever.

Normally, he ended the relationship, not the other way around. He shrugged. "Oh, well. You ended that, Mia."

While Marcy was a beautiful woman, they were a dime a dozen down at the club. Soon he'd find another.

"Women," he said, gazing down at the child. "This is

why I'll never marry. What am I going to do with you? Do you like sports? Football? How about cartoons? What is going to make you happy?"

The baby's bottom lip trembled and those eyes that he suddenly feared gazed at him. They were the same damn color as most of the Burnett men – startling blue eyes that gave them away.

How in the hell had Skylar had his child without telling him she was pregnant? No, she was just using him and she'd be lucky if he didn't call Child Protective Services on her.

But then he glanced down and gazed at the crying baby. What if she was his? And if his family learned about her, he would be in dog shit creek without a boat.

Opening the diaper bag, he glanced through the contents, not knowing what everything was for. Skylar hadn't given him instructions on what to do.

How could he keep this child through Sunday? Today was Friday. That would be two whole days.

"What do you need?" he asked the little girl who couldn't be more than three months old. "A clean diaper? A bottle? Tell me. A million dollars? Hell, I'd give you the ranch right now to keep you from crying."

Where was she going to sleep? He didn't have a crib.

He laid her on the carpet and then he went into the closet and came back with a fluffy blanket. Grabbing a baby blanket out of her bag, he laid a large quilt and then laid the child on her blanket.

"She said your name is Mia. Let's start with changing your diaper. Maybe that would make you stop crying." He took out a plastic-lined diaper from the bag.

He unsnapped the outfit she had on and pulled the wet diaper free.

"Can you please not poop until your mother returns," he told her. "My weak stomach won't be able to handle it, and where would I put the nasty diaper? It's not like we have trash pickup every day out here on the ranch. Just hold your poop."

The baby farted as if to reply *not happening*.

Those blue eyes gazed at him and he could see she wasn't certain about him. Lifting her legs, he slid the fresh diaper beneath her and then pulled the tabs hoping it was tight enough. At least he didn't get baby pee on him.

That would be gross.

"It would help if you could tell me if I was doing this right. You'll cry if I get it too tight. You'll wet on me if I get it too loose. I'm not cut out to be a babysitter or even a father. This is why I don't have children."

The baby stopped crying and gazed at him.

"Now what do we do?" he asked. "You're too young to drink, but I sure could use a whiskey right now."

She kicked her legs and he sat back on his heels and stared at her.

Was Mia his daughter? Was he a father?

"Damn, your mother has some questions to answer when she gets back here. In fact, I'm going to call her right now."

He picked up his phone and dialed Skylar's cell number which he still had in his contacts, miraculously.

"You have reached Skylar Beal. Joshua, you're her father, deal with her. I'm on my way to a fabulous shopping trip that will end with a party I'm attending on Saturday night. Sex for the first time in months. Don't call me again unless it's an emergency."

Click.

She'd changed her voice message just for him. Bitch.

Glancing down at the baby, he groaned. "Your mother comes from one of the richest families in Texas, why didn't she hire a nanny? Was this her way of getting revenge?"

The baby kicked her feet and then blew him a raspberry and his heart melted a little. She was cute.

But he didn't want marriage. He didn't want kids. He didn't want commitment. As a boy, he'd witnessed enough to make him positive he'd never get married.

Give him a woman like Marcy who only wanted mutual, gratifying sex and he was happy.

Suddenly the baby let out a squeal that quickly turned to tears.

"What's wrong? What do you need?"

Running his hand through his hair, he shook his head. Sure he'd had brothers, but they had been close together. He'd never been around babies much. He knew nothing.

Crying, she looked up at him, and he wanted to jump in his truck and race after her mother. But there was no way his truck could catch her Corvette.

He was a player, not a father, and he had no idea what

babies needed. And he hated her crying because it made him feel like he was failing her.

What the hell was he going to do?

Joshua

Contemporary Romance
Burnett Brides Contemporary Times
Travis
Tanner
Tucker
Joshua
Jacob
Justin
Cameron
Caleb
Cody
Desiree
Burnett Brides Contemporary Box Set Books 5-7
Burnett Brides Contemporary Box Set 8-10
Burnett Brides Contemporary Box Set 11-14

Return to Cupid, Texas
Cupid Stupid
Cupid Scores
Cupid's Dance
Cupid Help Me!
Cupid Cures
**Cupid's Heart
Cupid Santa
**Cupid Second Chance
Cupid Charmer
Cupid Crazy
Cupid's Bachelorette

Cupid Games
Return to Cupid Box Set Books 1-3
Cupid Help Me Box Set Books 4-6
Return to Cupid Box Set Books 7-9
Return to Cupid Box Set Books 10-12
**The Unlucky Bride

Contemporary Romance
My Sister's Boyfriend
The Wanted Bride
The Reluctant Santa
The Relationship Coach
Secrets, Lies, & Online Dating

Bride, Texas Multi-Author Series
**The Unlucky Bride

Coming Home for Christmas
I'll Be Home for Christmas
White Christmas
Santa's Baby
All I Want For Christmas
Box Set

Inheriting An Irish Groom
Inheriting a Scottish Castle

Kissing Oaks Billionaire Brothers
The Cowboy Billionaire's Lucky Break

The Cowboy Billionaire's Fate
The Cowboy Billionaire's Playbook
The Cowboy Billionaire's Secret
The Cowboy Billionaire's Deception
The Cowboy Billionaire's Match
Kissing Oaks Billionaire Brothers Box Set 1-3
Kissing Oaks Billionaire Brothers Box Set 4-6

Lipstick and Lead 2.0
Nailing the Hit Man
Nailing the Billionaire
Nailing the Single Dad
Box Set

Secrets of Mustang Island
Secrets of a Summer Place
Secrets of a Runaway Bride
Secrets From the Past
Secrets of a Reckless Life
Secrets of a Hidden Life
Secrets of a Midnight Letter

Secrets of Mustang Island Novellas
The Summer I Loved You
When We Meet Again
Christmas at Mustang Island

The Langley Legacy
Collin's Challenge

The Rancher Takes A Bride
The Outlaw Takes A Bride
The Marshal Takes A Bride
The Christmas Bride
Boxed Set

Lipstick and Lead Series
Desperate

Deadly

Dangerous

Daring

Determined

Deceived

Defiant

Devious
Lipstick and Lead Box Set Books 1-4
Lipstick and Lead Box Set Books 5-9
Lipstick and Lead Box Set Books 1-9
**Quinlan's Quest

Mail Order Bride Tales
**A Brother's Betrayal
**Pearl
**Ace's Bride

Scandalous Suffragettes of the West
**Abigail
Bella
Mistletoe Scandal

Southern Historical Romance
A Scarlet Bride

The Cuvier Women
Wronged
Betrayed
Beguiled
Boxed Set

The Debutante's of Durango
The Debutante's Scandal
The Debutante's Gamble
The Debutante's Revenge
The Debutante's Santa
Box Set

**** Denotes a sweet book.**

Want to learn about my new releases before anyone else? Sign up for my New Book Alert and receive a complimentary book.

USA Today Best-selling author, Sylvia McDaniel obviously has too much time on her hands. With over ninety western historical and contemporary romance novels, she spends most days torturing her characters. Bad boys deserve punishment and even good girls get into trouble. Always looking for the next plot twist, she's known for her sweet, funny, family-oriented romances.

Married to her best friend for over twenty-five years, they recently moved to the state of Colorado where they like to hike, and enjoy the beauty of the forest behind their home with their spoiled dachshund Zeus. (He has his own column in her newsletter.)

Their grown son, still lives in Texas. An avid football watcher, she loves the Broncos and the Cowboys, especially when they're winning.

www.SylviaMcDaniel.com
The End